This book belongs to

_____

My Big Book
of Bedtime Tales

This is a Parragon Publishing Book
First published in 2000 by Parragon

Parragon Publishing
Queen Street House
4 Queen Street
Bath BA1 1HE UK

Produced by the Templar Company plc
Pippbrook Mill
London Road
Dorking
Surrey RH4 1JE UK

Printed and bound in Indonesia
ISBN 0 75254 082 3

My Big Book
of Bedtime Tales

Retold *by* Stephanie Laslett

p

Contents

Nursery Tales

Wind in the Willows

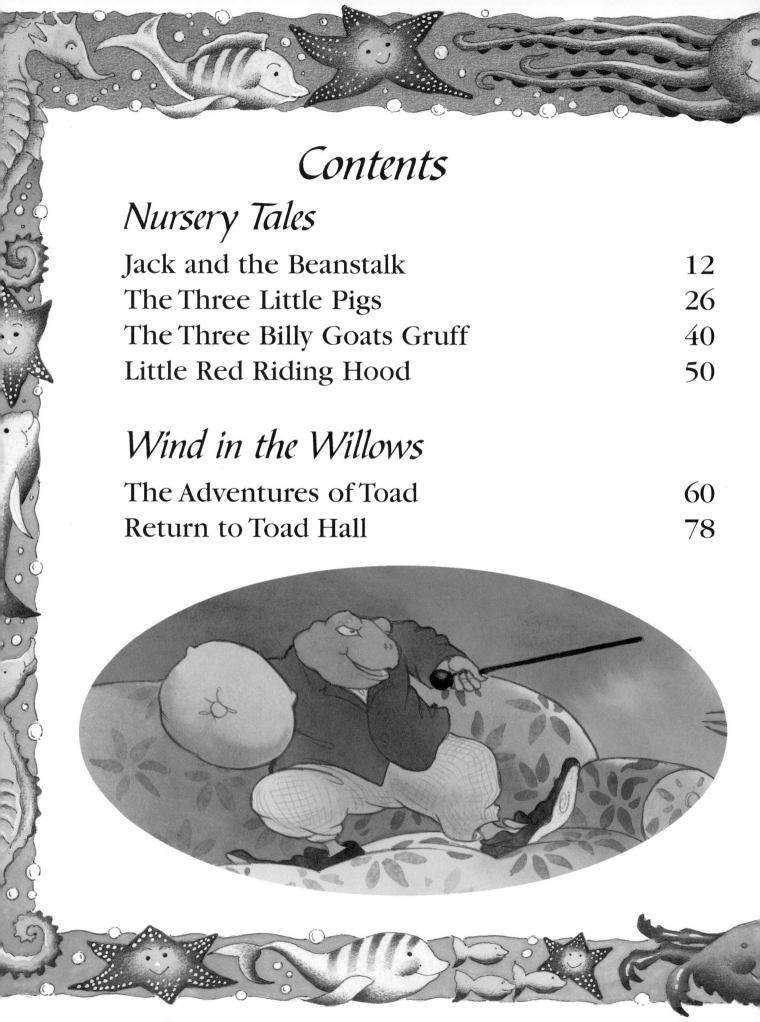

Aesop's Fables

Brer Rabbit

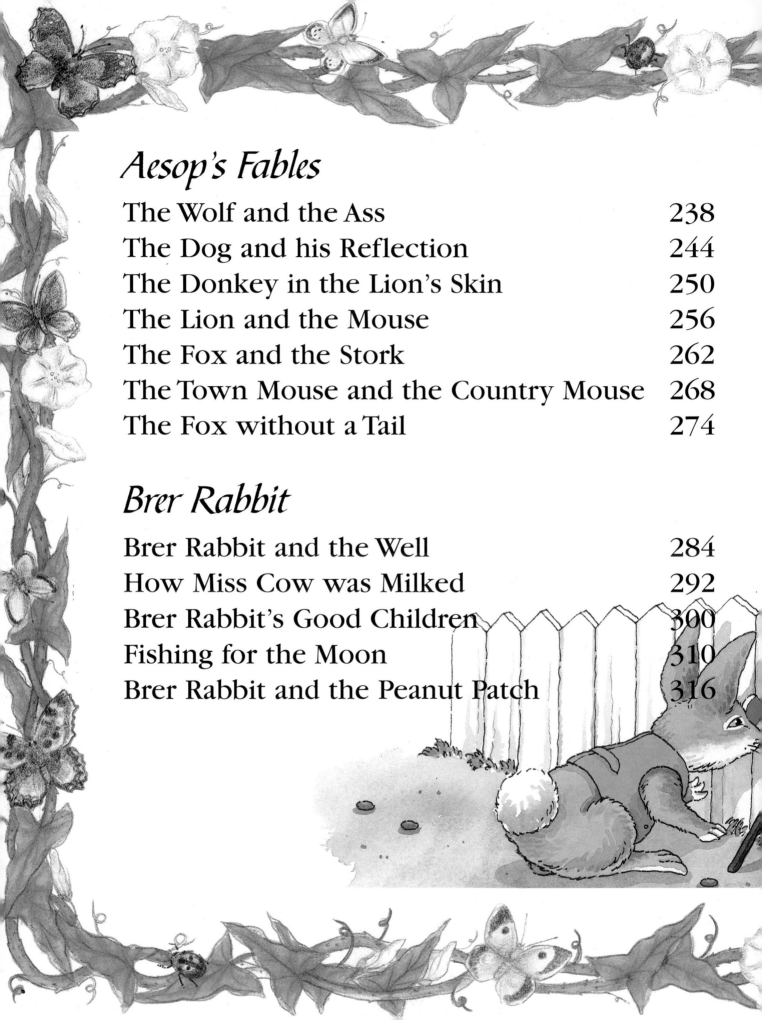

Arabian Nights

Nursery Tales

These old folk tales were handed down by word-of-mouth before appearing in print. They come from all over Europe, and were collected by storytellers in the seventeenth and eighteenth centuries. Some nursery tales have become familiar pantomime stories, part of the family Christmas tradition.

JACK AND THE BEANSTALK
Illustrated by David Anstey

Once upon a time there lived a poor widow woman and her son Jack. He was a lazy boy and he would not tend the crops in the field. Soon the plants died and then they had no food to eat.

"All we have left to sell is our cow," said Jack's mother, and so the next day Jack set off down the road to the market. After a while he met a pedlar.

"I will buy your cow," offered the pedlar, "and in return I will give you these special beans," and he held out his hand. Jack inspected the six speckled beans.

"It's a deal," said Jack and he hurried back home again.

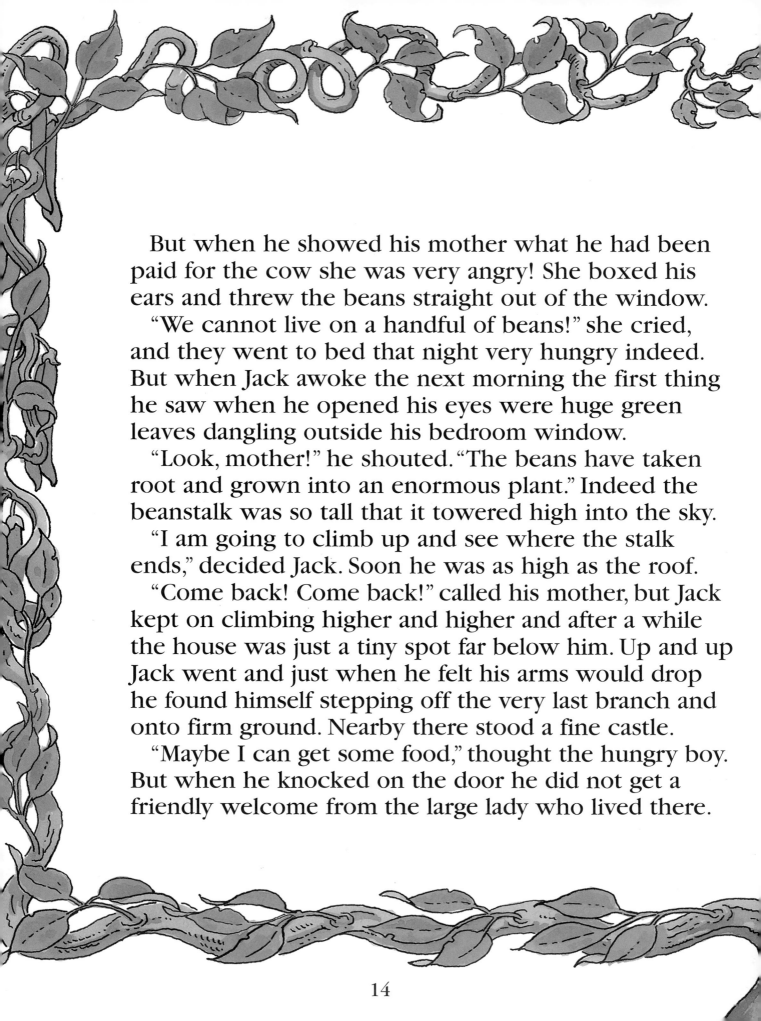

But when he showed his mother what he had been paid for the cow she was very angry! She boxed his ears and threw the beans straight out of the window.

"We cannot live on a handful of beans!" she cried, and they went to bed that night very hungry indeed. But when Jack awoke the next morning the first thing he saw when he opened his eyes were huge green leaves dangling outside his bedroom window.

"Look, mother!" he shouted. "The beans have taken root and grown into an enormous plant." Indeed the beanstalk was so tall that it towered high into the sky.

"I am going to climb up and see where the stalk ends," decided Jack. Soon he was as high as the roof.

"Come back! Come back!" called his mother, but Jack kept on climbing higher and higher and after a while the house was just a tiny spot far below him. Up and up Jack went and just when he felt his arms would drop he found himself stepping off the very last branch and onto firm ground. Nearby there stood a fine castle.

"Maybe I can get some food," thought the hungry boy. But when he knocked on the door he did not get a friendly welcome from the large lady who lived there.

"Go away!" she cried. "My husband is a fierce giant and he is particularly partial to small boys such as you." But Jack was so hungry that he begged to be allowed in, and at last the woman relented. Soon Jack found himself sitting at a huge kitchen table, happily nibbling a large piece of cheese. Suddenly the table shook and a loud roar filled the air.

"Fee, fi, fo, fum, I smell the blood of an Englishman!
Be he alive or be he dead,
I'll grind his bones to make my bread!"

"Quick, quick!" whispered the terrified woman. "You must hide for my husband is coming!" Hurriedly she bundled him into the oven and there Jack sat trembling like a leaf as the enormous giant strode into the kitchen and sniffed suspiciously.

"Hush, my dear. Don't fret! It is only the smell of your breakfast!" said his wife anxiously. "Come, sit and eat your food." Jack kept as quiet as a mouse as the giant shovelled the fried egg and bacon into his mouth.

"Now bring me my hen!" shouted the ogre.

The woman quickly fetched a small brown hen and placed it upon the table in front of him.

"Lay!" ordered the giant and to Jack's great astonishment the hen clucked loudly and instantly laid an egg. But this was no ordinary egg. No, this was a *golden* egg! The giant stroked the brown hen and smiled greedily. Then he yawned loudly, laid his great head upon his arms, and was soon fast asleep.

Jack was out of the oven and across the floor in a moment. Pausing only to grab the hen, he raced from the kitchen and out of the huge castle door. He ran for the beanstalk as fast as his legs could carry him and in no time at all he was back home with the hen still tucked tightly beneath his arm.

"Look, mother!" he cried. "This hen will lay as many golden eggs as we wish. We need never go hungry again."

But after a time Jack grew eager for adventure and decided to climb the beanstalk once more. The next day he dressed in a disguise and was soon up the beanstalk and knocking on the castle door.

The giant's wife looked at him suspiciously. "I foolishly admitted a small boy like you some months ago," she said, "and the ungrateful youth made off with my husband's favorite hen. I dare not risk letting you in." But Jack would not give up and so, once again, he found himself sitting at the giant's table. But what was this?

"Fee, fi, fo fum, I smell the blood of an Englishman!" The ogre was coming! Quickly Jack ran and hid in the oven. He peeked out as the ogre gulped down his meal.

"Bring me my money bags!" cried the giant when he had finished eating. Slowly he counted pile after pile of glittering golden coins but after a while he began to yawn and soon he was fast asleep. Jack jumped out of his hiding place, heaved a large money bag over his shoulder and ran like the wind away from the castle.

His mother was very thankful to see him safe and sound and what fun they had that night as they counted their new riches over and over again.

But after a time Jack grew restless and longed to visit the castle once more. His poor mother begged him to stay but all in vain for the next day Jack dressed in a different disguise and climbed the beanstalk.

This time the ogre's wife was more scared than ever.

"Some months ago another young fellow tricked me," she said. "He made off with my husband's money bag and oh! the trouble that caused me! The giant has been in a foul temper ever since."

But stubborn Jack would not be dissuaded and his fresh face looked so innocent that at last the poor woman gave in. But this time when Jack heard the giant's heavy footsteps thundering down the hall the oven was full of hot food and the only place that he could find to hide was inside the large washtub, surrounded by soapy socks.

The giant was indeed in a bad temper and he snarled and sniffed as he snooped around the kitchen. Under the bubbles, Jack shivered and kept as still as could be.

"What have we here?" the giant roared as he spotted the washtub. His wife wrung her hands nervously.

"Why, I am just washing your socks, dear," she said.

Luckily for Jack all giants hate water and with a grunt, the ogre turned aside and began to eat his meal.

"Bring me my harp!" he called to his wife as he threw down his last gnawed bone. In she hurried with a beautiful golden harp and it played the sweetest music Jack had ever heard. Soon the ogre was fast asleep and in a trice Jack leapt from the tub. He snatched up the harp and ran from the room but what a shock he got when the harp called out, "Master! Master!" With a cry of rage the ogre awoke and stumbled after little Jack. Out of the castle and down the beanstalk the terrified boy ran, with the giant close behind him all the way.

"Quick, mother, fetch the axe!" Jack shouted as he neared the ground. He swung the huge blade high in the air and with one mighty blow felled the plant. The giant gave a loud shriek, then tumbled from its branches and landed headfirst on the ground, stone dead.

And from that time on Jack and his mother enjoyed good luck and great happiness and Jack, having climbed the Ladder of Fortune and discovered that he had courage and an eager mind, was idle no more.

THE THREE LITTLE PIGS
Illustrated by Jenny Press

Once upon a time there were three little pigs. They lived at home with their mother but as the years passed they grew bigger and bigger and soon it was time for them to find homes of their own. Their mother kissed them and waved goodbye. "Watch out for the big, bad wolf!" she cried.

Soon they met a man carrying a bundle of straw.
"Please may I have some straw to build a house?" said the first little pig, and before long he was hard at work. The other two little pigs carried on down the road and after a while they met a man carrying a large bundle of sticks.

"Please may I have some sticks to build a house?" asked the second little pig, and soon he too was hard at work building a home for himself.

The third little pig carried on down the road and after a while he met a man carrying a load of bricks.

"Please may I have some bricks to build a house?" asked the third little pig, and soon he was very busy mixing cement and laying down brick after brick.

The first little pig finished his house of straw and shut the door. The second little pig finished his house of sticks and shut the door. The third little pig finished his house of bricks and shut the door.

"My house is good and strong," said each little pig to himself. "The wolf won't catch me now!"

The very next day who should come calling but the big, bad wolf! Down the road he prowled, peering under hedgerows and pouncing behind bushes. He was very hungry and he wanted something to eat.

When he saw the little straw house, he was most surprised.

"I wonder who lives here?" he said to himself and he peeked inside the window. How happy he was to see the first little pig sitting on the table and tucking into a large plate of porridge.

"Little pig, little pig!" he called. "Let me come in!"

The first little pig dropped his spoon in fright.
"No, no! By the hair of my chinny, chin, chin I
will *not* let you in!" he shouted.

"Then I'll huff and I'll puff and I'll blow your
house down!" roared the wolf. And he huffed and
he puffed and he *did* blow the house down and
in a trice he had eaten the first little pig all up.
Then he set off down the road. Soon he saw the
house of sticks and how delighted he was when
he spotted the second little pig sipping at a nice
cup of tea.

"Little pig, little pig, let me come in!" he cried.

"No, no! By the hair of my chinny, chin, chin I will *not* let you in!" shouted the second little pig.

"Then I'll huff and I'll puff and I'll blow your house down!" shouted the wolf and sure enough, the house blew down in no time at all and soon he had eaten the second little pig.

But when he visited the home of the third little pig he had a much harder job on his hands, for this house was made of bricks and however hard he huffed and puffed he could not blow it down. The wily wolf sat on the gate and tried to think of another plan to catch the clever little pig.

After a while the wolf knocked on his door.

"Oh, little pig," he called softly. "I know you like turnips and if you can be ready tomorrow morning at six o'clock then I will take you to Farmer Smith's field and help you pull some up." Well, the little pig was not going to fall for a trap like that and so he got up the next day and went to the field at *five* o'clock and was home cooking his turnips by the time the wolf knocked upon his door.

"You're too late," he called out. "I'm already cooking my dinner." Then the wolf gnashed his teeth and tried hard to think of another plan.

"Oh, little pig," he called. "I know you like apples so meet me at Merrygarden Farm at five o'clock in the morning and I will help you pick some." The next day the little pig went to the farm at *four* o'clock but the wolf, too, arrived early and caught him up a tree!

"Here, catch!" cried the clever pig, and he threw an apple across the meadow. The silly wolf went bounding after it and in a trice the pig was running for home. The wolf hid his anger and tried again.

"Meet me at the fair at three o'clock" he said.

But the pig went at *two* o'clock and bought a lovely butter churn. He was on his way home again when he saw the wolf coming up the hill towards him. There was nowhere to hide and so he jumped inside his barrel and rolled down the road. He thundered past the wolf and the noise frightened the poor beast so much that he turned tail and fled.

That evening the wolf knocked on the pig's door.

"A horrible monster attacked me today," he said in a quaky voice, and then the pig laughed and laughed.

"That was me in my butter churn!" he said. The wolf was furious and he climbed up on top of the roof.

"I am coming down your chimney to get you!" he cried. Quickly the pig put a large pot of water on his fire and as the wolf scrabbled down the chimney it boiled up good and hot. Splash! The wolf fell in the scalding water and was dead, but the pig lived happily ever after.

THE THREE BILLY GOATS GRUFF
Illustrated by Martin Aitchinson

Once upon a time in a land far away there lived three Billy Goats. There was a large Billy Goat, a middle-sized Billy Goat and a small Billy Goat. They were the Three Billy Goats Gruff.

They lived high up on a rocky mountainside and leapt from peak to peak in search of food. But they found very little grass and often went to sleep with their empty tummies rumbling with hunger.

"We will look for a better place to live," decided the oldest Billy Goat at last. "Somewhere with plenty of good, sweet grass to eat."

41

Soon they had reached the valley far below.

"That is the place for us," said the oldest Billy Goat and he nodded his head at a lush green meadow on the other side of a swift mountain stream. Now the only way to cross that stream was over a rickety wooden bridge and under that rickety wooden bridge lived the ugliest, fiercest troll that ever was. He liked nothing better than to gobble up goats for his supper. But the smallest Billy Goat Gruff stamped his hoof and set off over the bridge, trip, trap, trip, trap.

"Who's that trip-trapping over my bridge?" roared the troll and the little Billy Goat stood stock-still.

"It is me, the smallest Billy Goat Gruff," he said. "I am off to the meadow to eat the sweet grass."

"Oh, no, you are not!" roared the troll, "for I am going to eat you all up!"

"But I am small and bony," replied the smallest Billy Goat. "You should wait for my brother. He is much fatter than me." The troll scratched his head and the smallest Billy Goat Gruff quickly trotted over the bridge and was soon safe on the other side. Then the middle-sized Billy Goat Gruff began to cross the bridge.

"Who is that trip-trapping over my bridge?" roared the ugly, fierce troll.

"It is me, the middle-sized Billy Goat Gruff and I am off to the meadow to eat the sweet grass," he said.

"Oh, no, you are not! I am going to gobble you up!" cried the troll and he reared up from his hiding place.

"You don't want to do that," replied the Billy Goat. "You should wait for my big brother."

So the troll let the middle-sized Billy Goat past and waited for the largest Billy Goat Gruff to pass by. Soon he came trotting over the bridge, trip, trap, trip, trap.

"Who is that trip-trapping over my bridge?" roared the angry troll. "I am going to eat you all up!" But the biggest Billy Goat Gruff did not look at all afraid. He pawed the rickety wooden bridge with his strong hooves, lowered his head and then the troll suddenly spotted his two sharp horns — but it was too late! The big Billy Goat Gruff thundered towards him and his mighty horns butted the troll high into the air. He landed in the river with a loud splash and was never seen again. And the Three Billy Goats Gruff lived happily ever after in their lush meadow and grew very fat indeed!

LITTLE RED RIDING HOOD
Illustrated by Martin Aitchinson

Little Red Riding Hood set off one morning to visit her poor, sick Grandmamma. She carried a basket of sweet cakes and skipped happily along the forest path. Suddenly a big wolf stepped out from behind a tree and smiled at her. Now Little Red Riding Hood had never met a wolf before and so she was not afraid but the wicked wolf licked his lips and thought how nice it would be to eat this little girl all up.

"Where are you going?" asked the big, bad wolf.

"I am going to visit my Grandmamma," answered Little Red Riding Hood. "She lives in the cottage right in the middle of the wood."

"I will get there before her," thought the wolf to himself and off he ran. Soon he was peering inside the cottage window and there lay Grandmamma tucked up in bed. In a moment the wolf was through the door and had eaten her up, spectacles and all! Then he tied her lace bonnet over his head, crawled into bed and pulled the blankets up under his chin.

Soon Little Red Riding Hood arrived at the cottage and she knocked upon the door.

"Pull the cord to lift the latch," called the wolf and he sounded very like Grandmamma.

But when the little girl sat down beside the bed she was astonished to see how peculiar her Grandmamma looked in her nightclothes.

"Oh, Grandmamma, what big ears you have!" said Little Red Riding Hood.

"All the better to hear you with!" replied the wolf.

"Oh, Grandmamma, what big eyes you have!"

"All the better to see you with!" replied the wolf.

"Oh, Grandmamma, what big teeth you have!"

"All the better to eat you with!" cried the wolf as he leapt from the bed and he gobbled down Little Red Riding Hood in one mouthful.

Now, a little while later a woodcutter was passing by and he decided to pay Grandmamma a visit.

But what a shock he got when he found a great grey wolf fast asleep on her little bed. The woodcutter took one look at his fat tummy and guessed straightaway what had happened. With one swift stroke of his knife he cut the big bad wolf from chin to tail and out jumped Little Red Riding Hood.

"Where is your Grandmamma?" exclaimed the surprised woodcutter.

"Why, here she is!" replied Little Red Riding Hood and together they pulled the old lady out of the wolf. She lay on the bed and had soon recovered from her terrible ordeal. But the grim woodcutter looked at the wolf sternly. He must be punished.

"I will sew his stomach full of stones," decided the woodcutter. "That will teach him a lesson he won't forget!" Soon the job was done and when the wolf awoke he could hardly stand. His aching stomach felt as heavy as lead and try as he might he could not drag one foot in front of the other. The sorry-looking creature dropped dead on the mat and the woodcutter nodded his head, quite satisfied. Then they shared out the cakes and were never bothered by that big, bad wolf again!

Wind in the Willows

The tales of Mole, Ratty, Badger and Toad are amongst the most well-known of all stories created for children. They were written by Kenneth Grahame (1859-1932) for his son, and have since enchanted children all over the world. These two abridged stories are about the troublesome Toad.

ILLUSTRATED BY MAGGIE DOWNER

THE ADVENTURES OF TOAD

The winter passed slowly but at long last spring arrived. The Mole and the Water Rat were just finishing their breakfast when in strode the Badger. "The hour has come!" he announced solemnly. "I have just heard that another new motorcar has been delivered to Toad Hall. It is time for us to take Toad in hand!"

Soon the three of them were marching up the drive to Toad Hall. There stood the car — and there stood the proud Toad!

"Take the wretched creature inside," ordered the Badger, "while I explain to the driver that Mr Toad will no longer be needing this vehicle."

Toad was furious! The Mole and the Rat pulled off his driving clothes and soon he was locked in his bedroom. "It's for your own good, Toady," said the Rat kindly. "Soon you will see sense and thank us for it."

But Toad did not thank them. He knotted his bedsheets together, climbed out of his window and was soon marching briskly on his way.

After a while Toad reached a little town and there standing outside The Red Lion Hotel was the most beautiful green car. Toad was in raptures!

Next moment, hardly knowing how it came about, he found himself sitting in the driver's seat. As if in a dream he pulled the lever and swung the car onto the high road. As he tore through open countryside he shouted aloud for joy. "Make way! Make way for Toad, the Terror of the Road!"

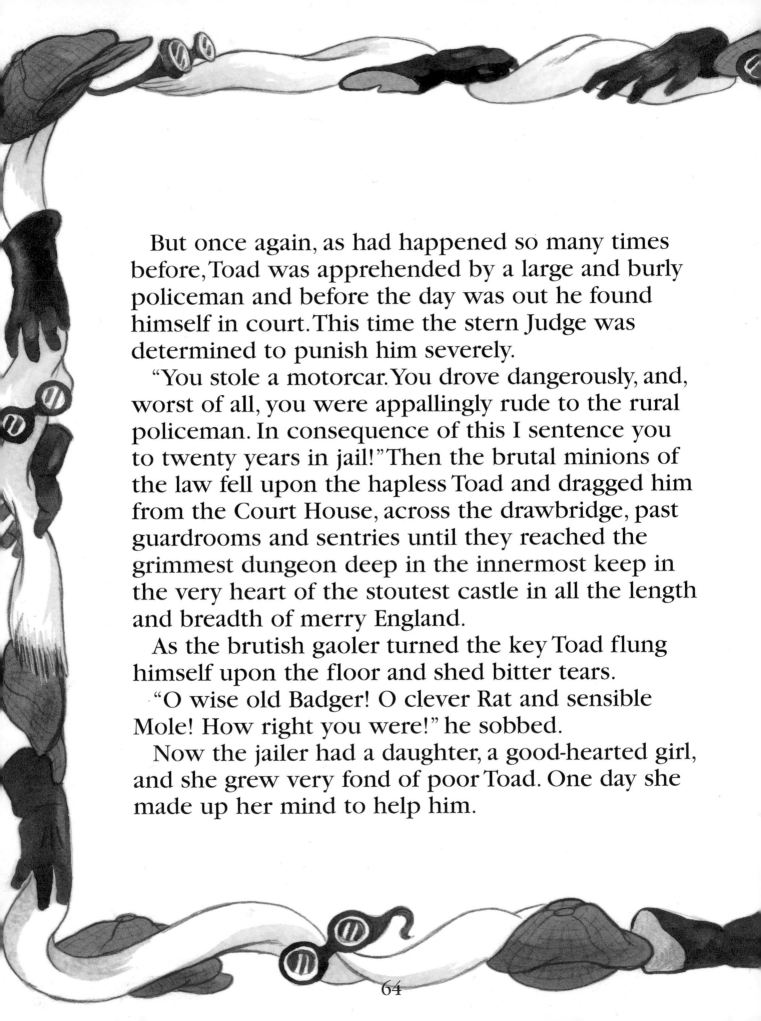

But once again, as had happened so many times before, Toad was apprehended by a large and burly policeman and before the day was out he found himself in court. This time the stern Judge was determined to punish him severely.

"You stole a motorcar. You drove dangerously, and, worst of all, you were appallingly rude to the rural policeman. In consequence of this I sentence you to twenty years in jail!" Then the brutal minions of the law fell upon the hapless Toad and dragged him from the Court House, across the drawbridge, past guardrooms and sentries until they reached the grimmest dungeon deep in the innermost keep in the very heart of the stoutest castle in all the length and breadth of merry England.

As the brutish gaoler turned the key Toad flung himself upon the floor and shed bitter tears.

"O wise old Badger! O clever Rat and sensible Mole! How right you were!" he sobbed.

Now the jailer had a daughter, a good-hearted girl, and she grew very fond of poor Toad. One day she made up her mind to help him.

"I have a plan," she told him. "My aunt is a washerwoman and she does all the washing for the prisoners. You and she are alike in many respects — particularly about the figure — so if you dress up in her clothes you could easily escape from the castle."

Toad thought this an excellent idea and in exchange for two gold sovereigns he received an old gown, an apron, a shawl and a black bonnet. At first the old lady hooted with laughter at the sight of Toad in her clothes but she soon stopped when she was bound and gagged in order to convince the jailer that Toad had overcome her.

With a quaking heart, Toad set forth but he was agreeably surprised to find that everyone he met was entirely convinced that he was indeed the washerwoman. Soon he was shutting the last door behind him. Free at last! He walked quickly towards the railway station but when he tried to buy a ticket at the ticket office he realised to his horror that he had no money on him. It was in his waistcoat back in the dungeon! Full of despair the poor Toad wandered down the platform to where the train was standing, and tears trickled down his nose.

The engine-driver caught sight of Toad and felt sorry for him. "What's the trouble, mother?" he asked.

"O sir!" cried Toad. "I am a poor washerwoman and I've lost my money, and I can't get home!" Well, the engine-driver was a good-hearted fellow and soon he had invited Toad to join him in the cab.

"You ride along with me," he said, but as soon as they left the station and were steaming along the track, the driver leaned out of his cab and looked puzzled. "There's another train close behind us," he said "and it looks as if it's chasing us!"

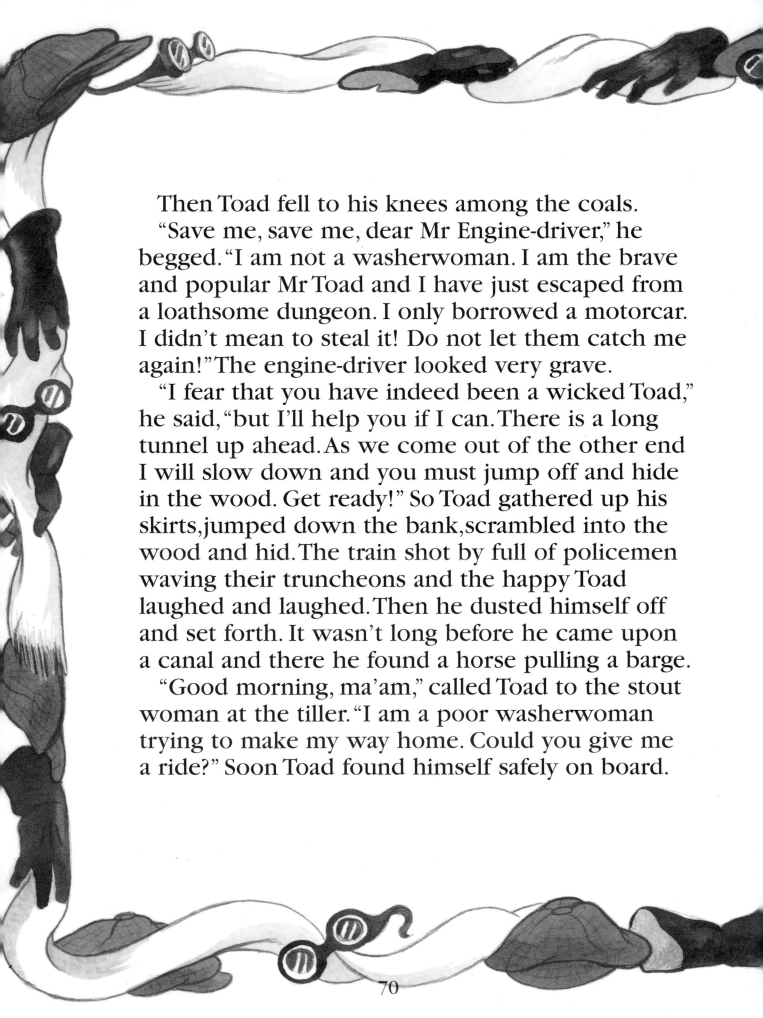

Then Toad fell to his knees among the coals.

"Save me, save me, dear Mr Engine-driver," he begged. "I am not a washerwoman. I am the brave and popular Mr Toad and I have just escaped from a loathsome dungeon. I only borrowed a motorcar. I didn't mean to steal it! Do not let them catch me again!" The engine-driver looked very grave.

"I fear that you have indeed been a wicked Toad," he said, "but I'll help you if I can. There is a long tunnel up ahead. As we come out of the other end I will slow down and you must jump off and hide in the wood. Get ready!" So Toad gathered up his skirts, jumped down the bank, scrambled into the wood and hid. The train shot by full of policemen waving their truncheons and the happy Toad laughed and laughed. Then he dusted himself off and set forth. It wasn't long before he came upon a canal and there he found a horse pulling a barge.

"Good morning, ma'am," called Toad to the stout woman at the tiller. "I am a poor washerwoman trying to make my way home. Could you give me a ride?" Soon Toad found himself safely on board.

"What a bit of luck, meeting you!" observed the barge-woman. "I have a whole heap of things to be washed. You can scrub my clothes while I steer the barge." Well, poor Toad had never washed a thing in his life and the barge-woman laughed aloud to see the dreadful mess he made of it.

"How dare you laugh at me!" shouted Toad. "I will have you know that I am the very well-known and distinguished Toad!" The barge-woman wrinkled her nose in disgust. "I will have no Toads on *my* barge!" she exclaimed and, catching him by the leg, she threw him overboard.

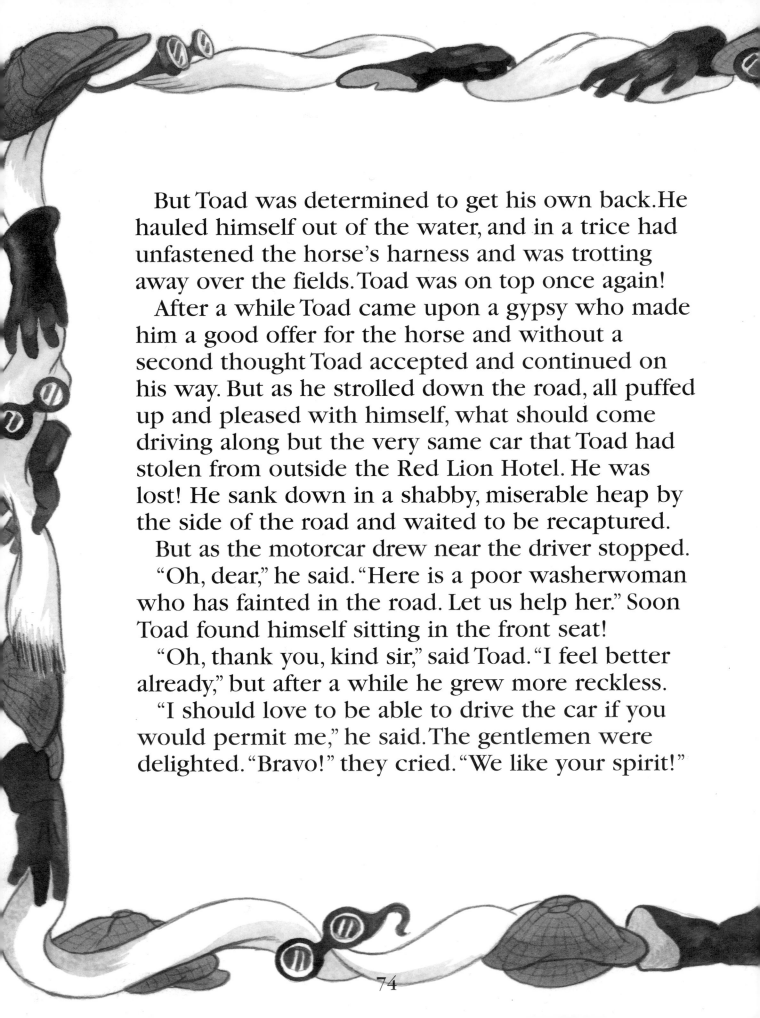

But Toad was determined to get his own back. He hauled himself out of the water, and in a trice had unfastened the horse's harness and was trotting away over the fields. Toad was on top once again!

After a while Toad came upon a gypsy who made him a good offer for the horse and without a second thought Toad accepted and continued on his way. But as he strolled down the road, all puffed up and pleased with himself, what should come driving along but the very same car that Toad had stolen from outside the Red Lion Hotel. He was lost! He sank down in a shabby, miserable heap by the side of the road and waited to be recaptured.

But as the motorcar drew near the driver stopped.

"Oh, dear," he said. "Here is a poor washerwoman who has fainted in the road. Let us help her." Soon Toad found himself sitting in the front seat!

"Oh, thank you, kind sir," said Toad. "I feel better already," but after a while he grew more reckless.

"I should love to be able to drive the car if you would permit me," he said. The gentlemen were delighted. "Bravo!" they cried. "We like your spirit!"

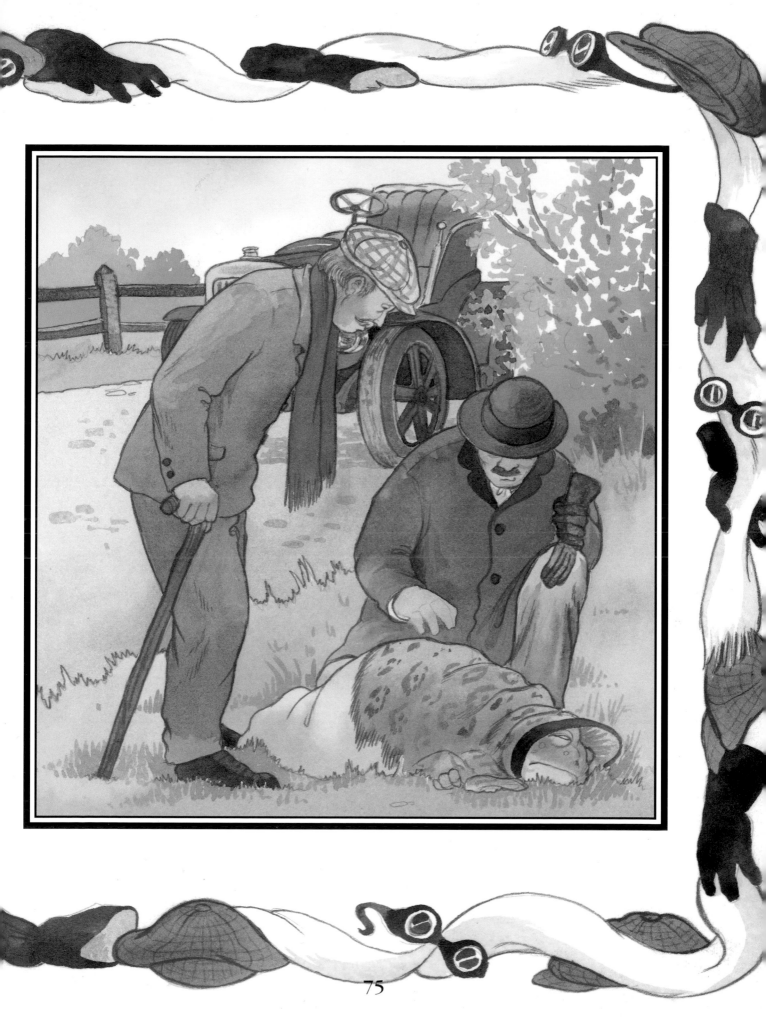

So it was that Toad found himself once more behind the wheel and then he began to lose his head.

"Ho, ho! I am the Toad," he cried. "The famous, the skilful, the entirely fearless Toad!" The horrified men flung themselves upon him and in a trice the car had crashed through a hedge and landed in a ditch.

Then Toad was off and running across country as hard as he could. He looked over his shoulder to where the men were hot on his trail and suddenly, splash! he found himself head over ears in deep, rapid water. He was swept along in the strong current until at last he managed to reach out and catch hold of a small hole in the bank. There he clung and after a while, to his great astonishment, a small brown face appeared. It was the Water Rat!

RETURN TO TOAD HALL

The Rat gripped the spluttering, waterlogged Toad by the scruff of the neck and pulled him inside. "Oh, Ratty!" cried Toad. "I've been through such times since I saw you last. Such sufferings!" But he got no sympathy at all from the exasperated Rat.

"Toad," he said sternly, "cars have brought you nothing but trouble. It grieves me to tell you that while you have been gallivanting all over the countryside the Wild Wooders have taken over Toad Hall!"

Then Rat told poor Toad the whole sorry tale.
"When the weasels and the stoats heard what had
happened to you, they got very cocky. One dark
night they armed themselves and broke into the
Hall and they have been living there ever since."
The tears welled up in Toad's eyes and fell to the
floor.

"We must talk to the Mole and Badger," declared
the Rat, and so that evening they all met up.

"It's no good," sighed the Mole. "There are sentries
and guns everywhere. We could never get in."

Then the Badger coughed. "I have a secret," he
said. "I know of an underground passage which will
take us up right into the middle of Toad Hall!"

"We shall creep out —," cried the Mole.

"— with our pistols and sticks —," added the Rat.

"— and whack 'em hard!" cried the Toad joyfully.

Now the very next day the Wild Wooders were going to have a party in Toad Hall and so, as the sounds of shouting and cheering rang far above them, the Brave Four crept along the secret tunnel. Soon they were under a trapdoor in the kitchen.

"The hour is come!" shouted the Badger.

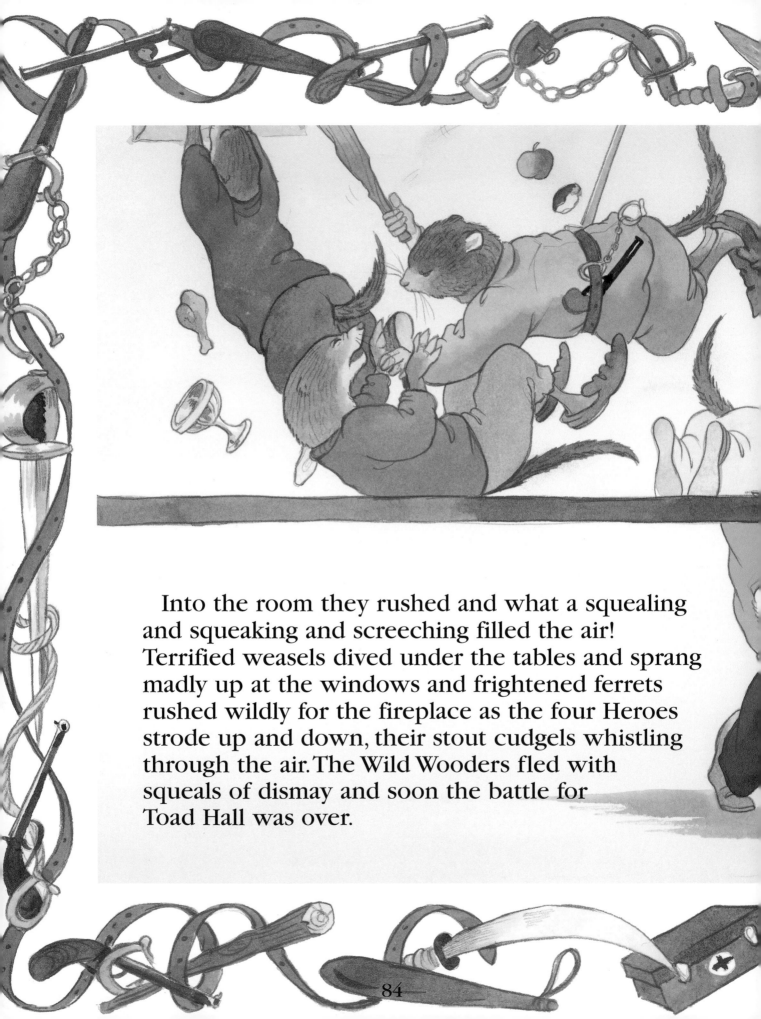

Into the room they rushed and what a squealing and squeaking and screeching filled the air! Terrified weasels dived under the tables and sprang madly up at the windows and frightened ferrets rushed wildly for the fireplace as the four Heroes strode up and down, their stout cudgels whistling through the air. The Wild Wooders fled with squeals of dismay and soon the battle for Toad Hall was over.

A great banquet was held in celebration of the victory and although Toad would very much have liked to fill the evening with his own speeches and songs, his friends persuaded him to reconsider and so the evening was judged a great success.

Indeed Toad seemed to turn over a new leaf and in time forgot his passion for cars altogether. On long summer evenings the four friends would stroll happily in the Wild Wood and it was pleasing to see how respectfully they were now greeted by the humble inhabitants. All was well once again!

Hans Christian Andersen

Hans Christian Andersen was born in Odense, Denmark on April 2nd, 1805. His family was very poor and he suffered much unhappiness throughout his life. Although his stories are often tinged with sadness, they have continued to be enjoyed by each new generation of children.

The Little Mermaid
Illustrated by Roger Langton

Far, far out to sea, where the water was deep and blue, the Mer People swam in their underwater grottoes. The Mer King had a fine palace made all of coral and there he lived with his six daughters. They loved their life under the sea but when the youngest daughter caught her first glimpse of the upper world, she thought it was the most wonderful place she had ever seen.

One evening the little Mermaid watched spellbound as a fine ship came sailing close by. She was near enough to see a young man in one of the cabins. He was a Prince and the Mermaid thought him the most handsome man in the world. Suddenly there was a loud clap of thunder and black clouds rolled across the sky. The wind whipped the waves as high as hills and, to the Mermaid's great terror, the great ship was struck by lightning and split right in two. The sea was full of men, all shrieking and wailing and there, clinging to a spar, was the handsome Prince. She took hold of his arm and, swimming strongly, towed him to land.

As he lay upon the beach a young girl found him and called for help. The Prince opened his eyes and believed that she was the one who had saved him. Only the little Mermaid, hiding behind a rock, knew the real truth. Before the Prince could ask who she was, the young girl ran off and so the Prince's rescue remained a mystery. But the little Mermaid could not forget him and every evening she swam to the surface of the sea and gazed at the palace where he lived.

"Come home with us," said her sisters, but the Mermaid longed to catch another glimpse of the Prince.

"You cannot share his life," they scolded. "You have a silver tail and will never be able to walk on dry land. You must forget him." But the Mermaid could think of nothing else. She would not be happy until she was rid of her tail and able to visit the upper world.

Far away, in a cave made from the bleached bones of shipwrecked sailors, there lived the Sea Witch.

"Perhaps she will be able to help me," said the little Mermaid to herself. "She frightens me dreadfully but I can think of no other way to win my heart's desire."

Through forests of slimy seaweed and across wild, frothing whirlpools the Mermaid swam until she reached the Witch's lair. The Witch listened to the little Mermaid's request as snails crept across her lap and a large green frog squatted upon her shoulder.

"I can take away your tail and give you those two stalks that men call legs," said the Witch at last, "but you will have to give me something in return. I want your sweet voice so I warn you, from the moment you drink my potion you will be struck dumb!" The Mermaid could think only of her Prince and agreed to this terrible demand at once.

"When you walk on land," added the Witch, "every step will be as if you are treading on sharp knives. Are you sure you want to endure this pain?" The Mermaid nodded quickly as she thought of her dear Prince and their life together in the upper world. Quickly she drank the magic potion and in a trice her tail turned into legs.

She found herself lying upon the marble steps beside the Prince's palace and when she was discovered by the Queen's maids she was dressed and brought before the royal family. They were all captivated by her beauty and sweet nature but when they asked who she was, the Mermaid could not say a word.

Gentle music filled the air and the Mermaid could not help but dance. She moved gracefully across the floor, spinning and twirling, but every step was agony and soon her eyes were filled with tears. The Prince held her in his arms and felt great pity and tenderness for the little girl but it was clear to the Mermaid that he did not share the same love that she had for him. As the weeks passed the Prince showed nothing but kindness to the Mermaid, but she longed for a love to equal her own.

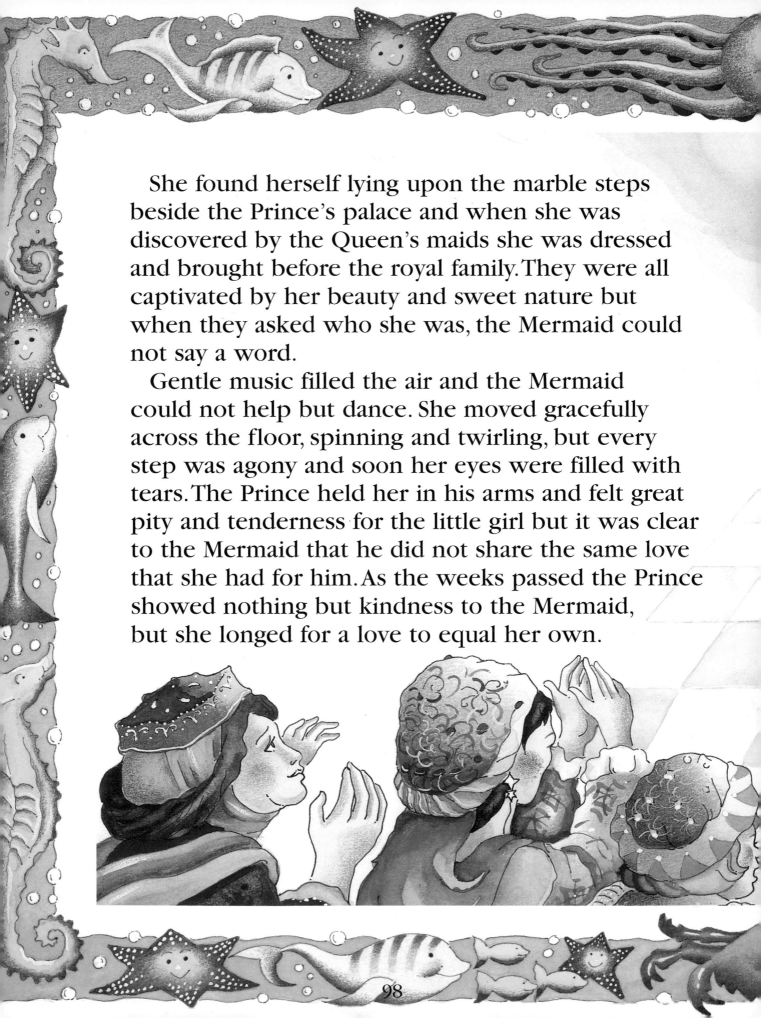

Soon the time came for the Prince to take a bride and the King and Queen announced that he would marry the daughter of a neighbouring king. As the Prince was introduced to the Princess the little Mermaid thought her heart would break for the girl was the same girl who had knelt by the Prince's side on the beach so long ago.

"You are the one who saved me!" cried the Prince, but the silent Mermaid could not explain the truth.

That night, as the happy couple slept aboard the royal ship, the little Mermaid looked sadly out to sea. All at once she saw her sisters rise up from the deep.

"Take this knife," they called. "The Sea Witch says that if you kill the Prince and let his blood fall upon your feet you will once again become a Mermaid!"

But as the Mermaid gazed upon his innocent face she knew she could never harm him and she threw the knife far overboard. Then, with one last look at her love, she jumped over the rail and into the foaming sea. She could feel herself melting away as she slowly became like the sea froth dancing above the crashing waves. Then, as a thousand sweet voices filled the air with song, she felt herself raised up high.

"Join us, little Mermaid," sang the voices. "We are the spirits of the air. We do not need the love of man for we can live forever." As she rose into the air, the Mermaid could see the Prince and his bride sleeping peacefully far below her and she was glad that they had found true happiness together. Then the Mermaid turned away, stretched out her gossamer arms, lifted her face to the sun and everlasting joy filled her heart.

The Ugly Duckling

Illustrated by Andrew Geeson

There was once a little mother duck. She had six eggs in her nest and there she sat day after day in the summer sun patiently waiting for them to hatch. Five of the eggs were small and white but the sixth egg was large and brown. The little duck often wondered why that egg was so different.

One morning she heard a crack, then another, then another. Her chicks were ready! One by one they tumbled from their shells and soon five little chicks were gathered under the wings of their proud mother. But the large brown egg had not hatched.

"What can be keeping my last little chick?" thought the mother duck to herself and she settled herself on top of the egg to keep it warm.

At last she felt the egg moving and out scrambled a chick. But this chick was nothing like her other babies. He was covered in dull brown fluff and had a long scrawny neck. He wasn't nearly as pretty as his brothers and sisters. But the mother duck loved him just the same and took care to protect him from the other farmyard animals who often teased him.

"Did you ever see anything quite as ugly as that gawky looking creature?" squawked a large brown duck to his friend, the white hen.

"Go away!" clucked the hen. "We don't want you in our farmyard," and she pecked at the poor little duckling with her sharp beak.

Not a day passed by without one animal or another making fun of the duckling so at last he decided he would run away. One dark night he crept away quietly while everyone was asleep and headed for the open fields. By daybreak he was quite exhausted.

"I will rest for a while," he said to himself and was soon fast asleep. But he awoke just two minutes later to feel the hot breath of a large animal wafting over him. Peeking out from under his wing he was terrified to see a fierce beast with a long red tongue! It was a hunting dog but to the duckling's great relief it simply sniffed him and then padded away across the moor.

"I am too ugly even for that dog to eat!" thought the duckling to himself sadly and he waddled off in search of somewhere to live. Not far away there was a cottage and for a time the duckling stayed there with an old lady, her hen and her cat. But they were not like him and as the days passed he longed to find some water so that he could splash about and swim.

"I must find a pond," he told the cat as he waved them goodbye. The weather grew colder and the snow began to fall. Suddenly the duckling heard a strange sound high above him and looking into the sky he saw a flock of white geese flying south for the winter.

The duckling watched them go, spellbound. He had never seen anything so beautiful in all his life.

"If only I could go with them!" he sighed, "but what would those lovely creatures want with an ugly companion like me."

On he trudged and at last he reached a little pond — but how wretched he was when he saw that the water had turned to ice! There was one small patch of freezing water and there he splashed for a while but the cold had sapped his strength. Soon he found he could not get out of the water and back onto the land. After a while the ice crept closer and closer and then he was trapped. The duckling would surely have died if a man had not happened to pass by at that very moment. He saw the little creature stuck fast in the ice and took him home and warmed him in front of the fire. So the duckling spent the next few weeks being cared for by the kind man and his wife.

Soon the weather grew warmer and the duckling longed to be on his way once again.

"I must find a proper home for myself," he explained to the man and his wife as he waddled away.

The air grew softer, the birds sang and the flowers bloomed in the meadows once again. The duckling felt stronger and he noticed that his feet and his body had grown much bigger and seemed to be changing color. He felt happy and excited and, stretching out his wings, he beat them up and down for fun. Just imagine his astonishment when he suddenly found himself leaving the ground and flying through the air! What a glorious feeling it was to be soaring on high.

"Here in the sky I am free!" he said to himself happily. All at once he saw something exciting far below him. As he swooped down to get a better look he recognised the snow white birds who had flown over him on their way south. Now they had returned and were splashing in the pond. The duckling landed on the water and slowly swam towards them.

"I know I am ugly," he said shyly, "but please let me stay with you and be your friend."

"Why, you are not ugly!" laughed the birds. "You have become a beautiful swan just like us," and as the duckling bowed his head to look in the water he saw that it was indeed true!

The Steadfast Tin Soldier

Illustrated by Helen Smith

There was once a Tin Soldier. He was exactly the same as his twenty-four brothers, but for one thing. He had only one leg! When he was made, the tin ran out just as it was about to be poured into his second leg, but he could still stand straight and tall.

He lived in the nursery with all the other toys but his favorite by far was a pretty little lady who stood on one toe and pointed her other foot high in the air. Why, it was almost as if she had only one leg, just like him! She was made all of paper and held her arms gracefully above her head, for she was a Dancer.

The Steadfast Tin Soldier loved to watch her and stood perfectly still for hour after hour gazing at her lovely face and wishing he could speak to her.

"But what is the use of trying to win her love?" he sighed. "She lives in a grand castle and I have to share a wooden box with my twenty-four brothers."

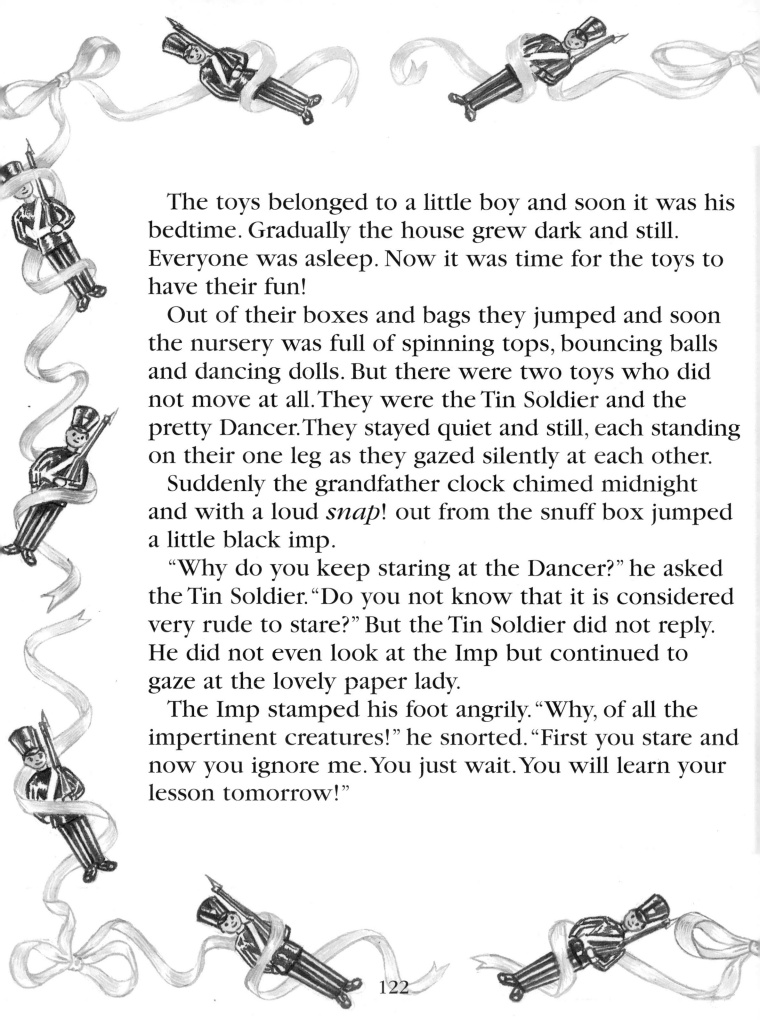

The toys belonged to a little boy and soon it was his bedtime. Gradually the house grew dark and still. Everyone was asleep. Now it was time for the toys to have their fun!

Out of their boxes and bags they jumped and soon the nursery was full of spinning tops, bouncing balls and dancing dolls. But there were two toys who did not move at all. They were the Tin Soldier and the pretty Dancer. They stayed quiet and still, each standing on their one leg as they gazed silently at each other.

Suddenly the grandfather clock chimed midnight and with a loud *snap*! out from the snuff box jumped a little black imp.

"Why do you keep staring at the Dancer?" he asked the Tin Soldier. "Do you not know that it is considered very rude to stare?" But the Tin Soldier did not reply. He did not even look at the Imp but continued to gaze at the lovely paper lady.

The Imp stamped his foot angrily. "Why, of all the impertinent creatures!" he snorted. "First you stare and now you ignore me. You just wait. You will learn your lesson tomorrow!"

The next day the little boy played with the one-legged Tin Soldier and when he went for his tea he left him standing on the windowsill. Now whether it was the wind or whether it was the little black imp up to his tricks, who can say, but all of a sudden the window flew open and the Soldier was blown outside!

Down he tumbled and with a bump landed upside down between two paving stones. There he stayed, firmly wedged, while the little boy searched high and low. If only the soldier had called out he would have been found in an instant but he was proud and felt that no soldier should have to call for help. The little boy returned indoors and soon it began to rain. The raindrops fell faster and faster and before long there was a real downpour.

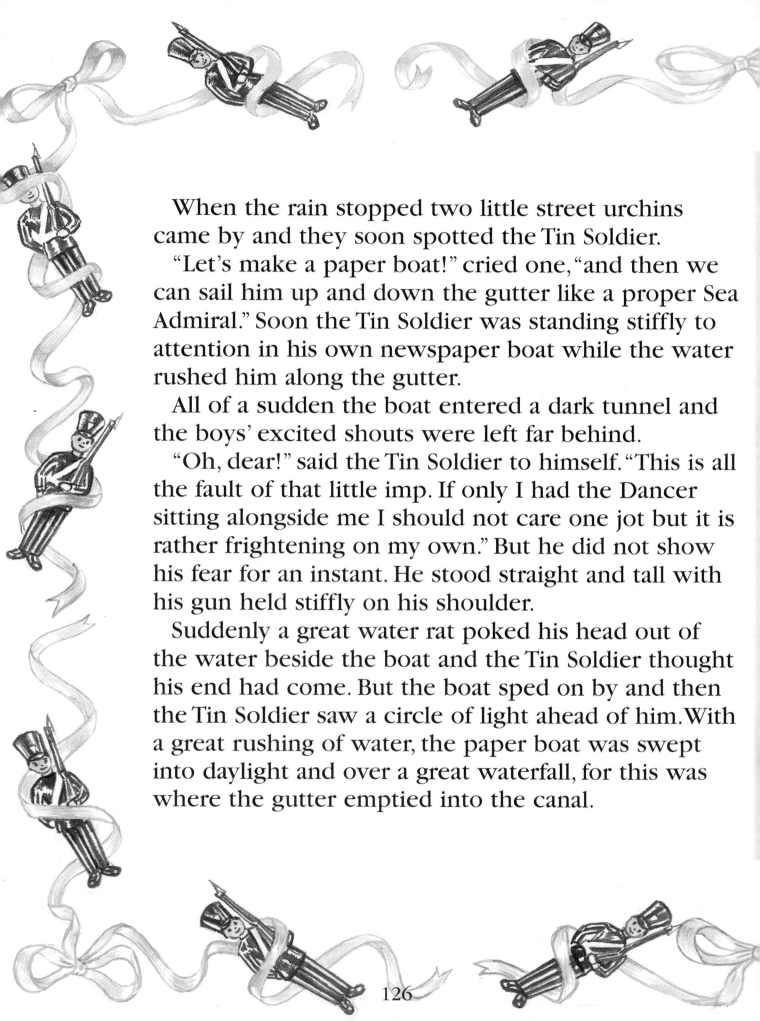

When the rain stopped two little street urchins came by and they soon spotted the Tin Soldier.

"Let's make a paper boat!" cried one, "and then we can sail him up and down the gutter like a proper Sea Admiral." Soon the Tin Soldier was standing stiffly to attention in his own newspaper boat while the water rushed him along the gutter.

All of a sudden the boat entered a dark tunnel and the boys' excited shouts were left far behind.

"Oh, dear!" said the Tin Soldier to himself. "This is all the fault of that little imp. If only I had the Dancer sitting alongside me I should not care one jot but it is rather frightening on my own." But he did not show his fear for an instant. He stood straight and tall with his gun held stiffly on his shoulder.

Suddenly a great water rat poked his head out of the water beside the boat and the Tin Soldier thought his end had come. But the boat sped on by and then the Tin Soldier saw a circle of light ahead of him. With a great rushing of water, the paper boat was swept into daylight and over a great waterfall, for this was where the gutter emptied into the canal.

The water hissed and boiled around the little boat and the flimsy paper could take no more. It slowly fell apart and the Tin Soldier sank below the surface, still standing proudly to attention. As the water slid over his head all he could think of was the peaceful face of the little Dancer.

Suddenly the Tin Soldier heard a loud *gulp*! and to his great surprise found himself in total darkness. He had been swallowed by a fish! After a short while the fish began to twist this way and that and just when the Tin Soldier felt he could bear it no longer, all was still once again. There he lay shouldering his gun and wondering what on earth was to become of him.

The hours passed and just when the Tin Soldier truly believed he was lost forever there came a blinding flash of light and he found himself lying on a table.

The Tin Soldier had had quite a journey. The fish had been caught on a hook and taken to market. There it had been bought and was now lying silver-bright on a kitchen table, ready to be cooked.

"Why, it's a little Tin Soldier," exclaimed the cook.

"I will take him upstairs to the nursery."

So it was that the little Tin Soldier found himself standing on a table and looking into the face of a little boy. Well, what strange things do happen in this world! He was in his old nursery and there was the pretty Dancer still standing on one toe the same as she always did.

But the boy was not pleased to see the Tin Soldier. Maybe it was because he looked so shabby, or maybe the little black imp had something to do with it, but he snatched up the Tin Soldier and threw him in the fire!

There he stood, as brave as could be, and the flames flickered around him. He looked straight at the paper lady and she looked right back at him.

Suddenly the door opened and a draught picked the paper lady off the table and carried her through the air. Straight towards the fire she floated and there she landed right in the arms of the Tin Soldier. As her arms brushed his cheek she burst into flames and was gone. Then the Tin Soldier finally melted.

The next morning when the maid swept out the fire she found a cinder of black paper and a small lump of tin in the shape of a heart — all that was left of the Dancer and her Steadfast Tin Soldier.

The Swineherd
Illustrated by Annabel Spenceley

There was once a Prince who decided he would find himself a bride. He had his heart set on marrying the Emperor's daughter and so he sent two special gifts to win her love. In one casket was a rose blossom with a scent that was sweet enough to make you forget all your cares and sorrows and in the other casket perched a little nightingale with a song that would make your heart sing.

But when the Emperor's daughter saw these treasures she stamped her foot and sent them away.

"What do I want with a silly flower and a brown bird?" she pouted. "I prefer jewels and toys." But the Prince would not give up so easily and, dressed as a peasant, he went to the Emperor and asked for work.

"The only job I have is for a Swineherd," replied the Emperor. "You will find your lodgings with them." And so the Prince was made Imperial Swineherd and given a horrid little room next to the pigsties in which to live.

He worked busily all day and soon he had made a beautiful little cooking pot.

If you held your finger in the steam you could smell what everyone in the palace was cooking for their dinner, from the Lord Chancellor's roast beef right down to the scullery maid's thin gruel.

The next day the Princess came by and when she heard the magical, musical pot she sent her lady-in-waiting to ask what it would cost. What a shock!

"The Swineherd is asking for ten kisses from Your Royal Highness!" the maid gasped. The Princess was outraged by this impertinence but the more she thought of the pot, the more she wanted it and so at last she gave in and the Swineherd took his ten kisses.

The magic pot was a great success but the Swineherd did not stop there. He set to and made a singing rattle and when he swung it around his head it played the jolliest of waltzes and polkas. When the Princess heard the rattle she was determined to make it hers. But how dismayed she was to hear that this time the naughty Swineherd wanted a hundred kisses!

"It is a terrible thing for the Emperor's daughter to be seen kissing a Swineherd," said the Princess, "but I must encourage a true artist and so I will do as he asks."

From his window the Emperor could see a little crowd clustered in front of the pigsties.

"What are the ladies-in-waiting up to now?" he said. "I will tiptoe up behind them and find out." Softly, softly he crept into the pig yard and there he saw his beloved daughter in the arms of the filthy swineherd!

"What is the meaning of this?" he thundered as he fell about the Swineherd with his slipper. "You are both banished from the palace!" and the poor Princess and the disguised Prince were locked outside the gates.

"Now what is to become of me?" wailed the forlorn Princess. "If only I had married that Prince while I had the chance." Then the Swineherd went behind a tree and changed out of his dirty clothes. When he next stepped before her he was dressed as a fine Prince and the Princess blushed and curtsied prettily in front of him.

But the Prince was not impressed. "You did not appreciate my gifts of the rose and the nightingale," he said sternly, "but you would kiss the Swineherd for a silly musical pot! You have made your bed and now you must lie in it!"

And so the Prince returned to his own kingdom and left the Princess with only a pot and a rattle for company.

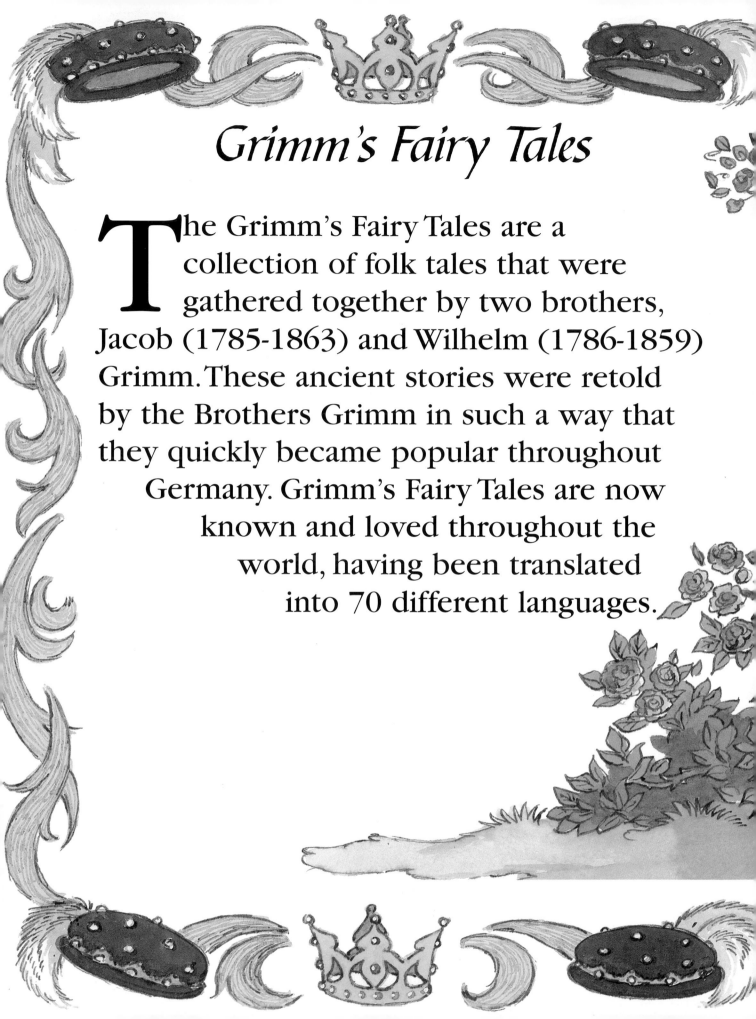

Grimm's Fairy Tales

The Grimm's Fairy Tales are a collection of folk tales that were gathered together by two brothers, Jacob (1785-1863) and Wilhelm (1786-1859) Grimm. These ancient stories were retold by the Brothers Grimm in such a way that they quickly became popular throughout Germany. Grimm's Fairy Tales are now known and loved throughout the world, having been translated into 70 different languages.

Hansel and Grettel
Illustrated by Annabel Spenceley

Once upon a time long ago there lived a poor woodcutter and his two children, Hansel and Grettel. The children's mother had died when they were very young and their father had married again. Their stepmother was a wicked woman and she did not love Hansel and Grettel. The woodcutter had very little money to spend on food and so all four of them went hungry for much of the week.

Late one night as the two children lay shivering in their beds they heard their stepmother talking.

"Something must be done or we will all starve to death," the woman whispered to the children's father. "We have enough food for two mouths, but not for four. We must get rid of Hansel and Grettel."

Grettel wept bitterly as she heard her stepmother describe how she would lead the children deep into the forest and leave them there to perish.

"I will find a way home, little sister," said Hansel.

The next morning the children were taken far away.

"Stay here until we return," said their stepmother.

Soon night fell and they were left quite alone.

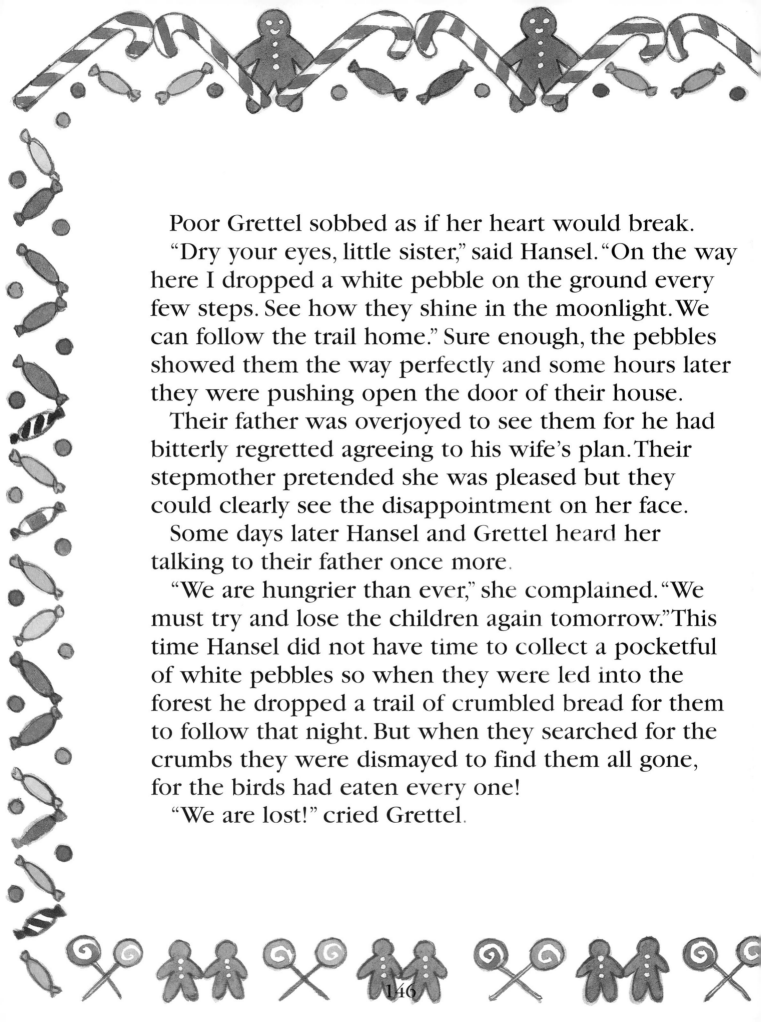

Poor Grettel sobbed as if her heart would break.

"Dry your eyes, little sister," said Hansel. "On the way here I dropped a white pebble on the ground every few steps. See how they shine in the moonlight. We can follow the trail home." Sure enough, the pebbles showed them the way perfectly and some hours later they were pushing open the door of their house.

Their father was overjoyed to see them for he had bitterly regretted agreeing to his wife's plan. Their stepmother pretended she was pleased but they could clearly see the disappointment on her face.

Some days later Hansel and Grettel heard her talking to their father once more.

"We are hungrier than ever," she complained. "We must try and lose the children again tomorrow." This time Hansel did not have time to collect a pocketful of white pebbles so when they were led into the forest he dropped a trail of crumbled bread for them to follow that night. But when they searched for the crumbs they were dismayed to find them all gone, for the birds had eaten every one!

"We are lost!" cried Grettel.

Again and again they tried to find a way out of the forest but every path they took led them ever deeper into the wood. Suddenly Hansel saw a white dove sitting upon a branch. She twittered at them, then flew off over the trees.

"I believe she is telling us to follow her," said Hansel and with weary steps they trudged after the little bird. She sang as if to encourage them on their way and after a time they found themselves in an open glade. And there in the middle of the clearing was the most perfect little gingerbread cottage.

"Oh, Hansel!" gasped Grettel. "The roof is made of honey cake and the windows are made of barley sugar! I must just nibble a little corner." Soon they were both munching away on their favorite bits of the house and nothing had ever tasted quite so delicious.

All of a sudden the door flew open and out hobbled an old dame leaning upon a stick. The children drew back in fear but the old lady smiled at them kindly.

"Welcome to my home, my dears," she said. "Come inside and I will look after you." She fed them sweet pancakes, then put them to bed under cosy quilts.

But when Hansel and Grettel awoke next day the old lady's kind manner had changed. Her weak eyes glinted cruelly as she grabbed Hansel by the arm.

"You will make a tasty morsel for me to eat," she cackled and then the children saw that they had been tricked. The old lady was a witch and she meant to make a meal of them! Laughing cruelly, she bundled Hansel into a cage.

"I will fatten you up before I cook you," she hissed and Hansel shook with fear. Every day she checked to see how fat he was getting but clever Hansel stuck an old bone through the bars and when the old crone pinched it, she decided he was still too thin to eat.

At last the witch could wait no longer.

"Fat or thin, I will eat him as he is," she decided, clutching at Grettel with one claw-like hand. "And you will help me prepare the cooking pot."

How the little girl sobbed as she carried the water and lit the fire under the oven. The witch scowled at her and stamped her feet.

"Stop your wailing," she shouted. "Just climb in the oven and tell me how hot it is." Then Grettel had a clever idea. She looked up at the Witch timidly.

"I don't know how to climb inside the oven," she said anxiously. "Can you show me?"

The witch stamped her foot again, but moved close to the oven entrance.

"Why, you silly goose," she said crossly, "it is perfectly simple. All you have to do is put one foot here and then you can step right inside." But as the witch showed her where to put her feet Grettel suddenly ran at her and with a great shove pushed the old hag right inside the oven and slammed the iron door tight shut. Gracious, how the old witch yelled! Soon Hansel was free from the cage and jumping for joy.

Then the two children explored every inch of the gingerbread cottage, upstairs and down and hidden in every corner were chests full of treasure. Jewels and pearls, gold and silver — the children could hardly believe their eyes! They filled their pockets to the brim and little Grettel held as much as she could hold in her apron.

Soon they were ready and they set off to find their way home. After a while they came to a large lake but they could find no way of crossing the water.

"Now we will never see Father again," sighed Hansel, but just then a large white duck came swimming by.

"I will carry you over on my back," she offered and so the two grateful children were delivered safe to the other side. For many hours they walked under the shade of the trees and after a time the forest began to look more familiar and then, to their delight, Hansel and Grettel saw their own little home in front of them.

Their father wept for joy as he gathered the children into his arms for he had not had a single happy hour since he had lost them.

"Your wicked stepmother has gone away for good," he said. "Now we will be together forever.

The Golden Goose
Illustrated by Claire Mumford

Once upon a time there were three brothers. The youngest son was given the name of Dummling and was laughed at by his family and everyone else.

One day the eldest son went into the forest to cut some wood. His mother gave him cake and a bottle of wine and off he went, whistling cheerfully. But he had no sooner set to work than a little old man appeared.

"I am so hungry and thirsty. May I have some cake and wine?" he asked. But the eldest son shook his head.

"Be off with you," he said gruffly. "I will share my meal with no-one." But it seemed the old man was going to get his revenge with the very next swing of the ax for it landed on the eldest son's foot. How he yelled! The next day the second son decided to try his luck and once again his mother gave him cake and wine.

The little old man approached the second son and asked to share his meal, but the second son also refused. He, too, was cut by the next swing of the ax.

The next day Dummling set off for the forest to cut some wood. He was given only bread and water but was happy to share what he had with the little man.

"You are a good boy," said the man, "and if you cut down that tree you will get your reward." Dummling did as he was bid and was astonished to find a goose covered entirely with golden feathers.

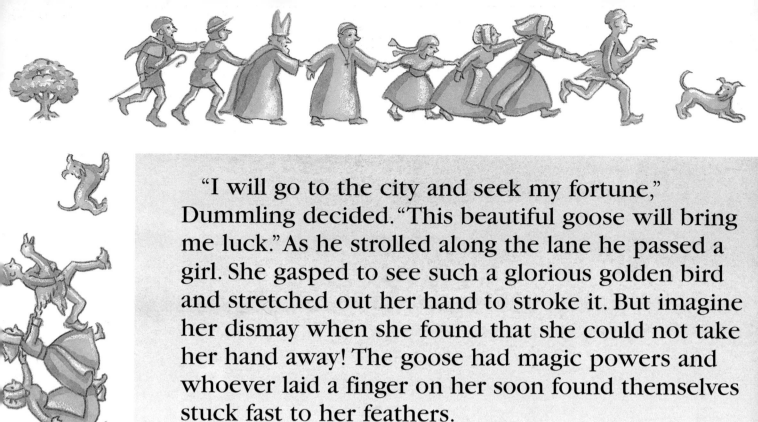

"I will go to the city and seek my fortune," Dummling decided. "This beautiful goose will bring me luck." As he strolled along the lane he passed a girl. She gasped to see such a glorious golden bird and stretched out her hand to stroke it. But imagine her dismay when she found that she could not take her hand away! The goose had magic powers and whoever laid a finger on her soon found themselves stuck fast to her feathers.

Before many hours had passed Dummling had collected two more inquisitive girls and a Parson, all stuck fast one behind the other. As they stumbled across the fields they met the Bishop.

"My dear Parson!" he cried. "Have you taken leave of your senses?" and he reached out and caught the Parson's sleeve. Now he, too, was stuck fast and it wasn't long before they were joined by a plowman and a shepherd!

After a time they reached the city and there in the palace lived the King and his daughter. She had never been known to smile and the King had promised her hand in marriage to the first person who was able to make her laugh. Well, when the Princess saw the three girls, the Parson, the Bishop, the plowman and the poor shepherd all falling over one another behind Dummling's golden Goose, she burst into peals of laughter.

The King came running and Dummling lost no time in asking permission to marry the Princess.

"Hmm," thought the King to himself. "I do not want this raggle taggle boy to marry my daughter. I must set him an impossible task to perform and when he fails, I will be able to refuse him."

And so the King told Dummling that before the marriage could take place he would first have to find a man who could drink a whole cellarful of wine.

Dummling scratched his head and then he remembered the old man in the forest. But when he returned to the glade the old man was not there. Instead, he found a short man with a miserable face.

"Oh, my, I am so terribly thirsty," he moaned. "I have already drunk a barrel of wine but I feel as if I could drain a lake dry!"

"You are just the man I am looking for!" cried Dummling and he led the man to the King's cellar.

The fat man rubbed his hands with glee.

"This is a sight for sore eyes!" the short man declared and soon he had emptied every bottle, keg, cask, and barrel. The King was more vexed than ever. He decided to set another task and this time made it even harder.

"Find me a man who can eat a whole mountain of bread," he ordered, well satisfied that this would indeed prove impossible.

But Dummling went straight to the forest and there discovered a tall, thin man sitting on a log.

"I have just had four ovenfuls of bread for my supper but it has barely taken the edge of my appetite," he complained. Dummling pulled at his sleeve.

"I know a place where you can eat your fill," he said.

When he arrived back at the Palace the cooks set to work and kneaded their dough for a day and a night. When the bread was piled high it filled the whole courtyard!

The tall, thin man ate and ate and ate and within hours the mountain had become a molehill, and soon there was nothing left at all.

Then the King set one last impossible quest.

"Find me a ship which can sail both on land and on sea. Only then can you marry my daughter," he declared.

This time Dummling found the little old man waiting for him in the forest.

"I have not forgotten your kindness," he said. "Now look behind you." Then, with a great rustling of canvas, the most magnificent ship sailed into the glade.

When the King saw the ship sailing over the fields towards his palace he knew he would have to give in and so Dummling and the Princess were married.

They lived happily ever after but back at home Dummling's two brothers grew bitter and miserable — and all for the lack of a good, generous heart.

Rapunzel

Illustrated by Annabel Spenceley

There once lived a man and his wife. They were good, simple people but they were not happy for they longed for a child. At last the woman grew so sad that she fell ill and took to her bed. From her window she could see into the garden of the big house that stood next door. This house belonged to a witch and the garden was surrounded by a high wall so everyone kept well away. But the more the woman gazed into that garden, the more she longed to taste the fresh, green herb that grew there.

"You must fetch me some of that rampion herb to eat or I shall surely die!" she said at last to her husband. So one night when all was dark the man climbed the wall and hastily gathered a handful of leaves. Soon he was back home, safe and sound and as his wife tucked into the herb she began to feel much better.

But as the days passed she fell ill a second time and begged her husband to fetch her more of the health-giving herb. So it was that he climbed the wall again. But this time the witch was waiting!

"How dare you creep into my garden and steal my rampion like a common thief?" she demanded.

The poor man fell to his knees, covered his eyes and quivered like a leaf.

"Forgive me!" he begged. "My wife could see the plant from her window and it looked so good that she longed to taste it." This compliment softened the witch a little, but then her eyes grew cunning.

"I shall let you go free on one condition," she hissed. "Your wife will soon have a baby but when it is a week old you must give it to me." The man was so terrified that he would have agreed to anything.

"Yes, yes," he gasped and without a backward look he scrambled over the wall and ran for home.

Some months after this, his wife did indeed have a baby daughter and great was their joy. But on the seventh day after her birth the witch swept into the room, plucked the child from the cradle and was gone! The man and his wife were grief-stricken but however hard they searched, they never saw the witch or their daughter again.

The witch raised the little girl all alone and named her Rapunzel, for that is another name for the rampion plant. When Rapunzel was sixteen the witch locked her away in a tall tower in the middle of the forest and each day she would visit her and call out:

"Rapunzel, Rapunzel, let down your golden hair!"

Then Rapunzel would let her long plaits fall from the window and the witch would hold on and climb up hand over hand.

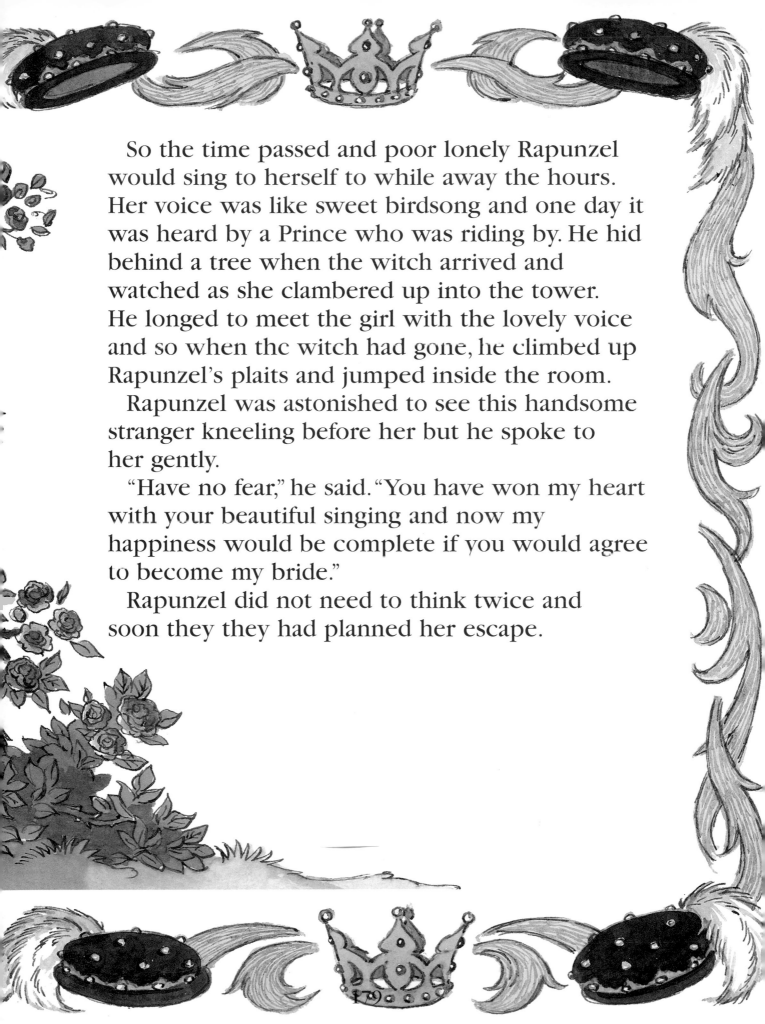

So the time passed and poor lonely Rapunzel would sing to herself to while away the hours. Her voice was like sweet birdsong and one day it was heard by a Prince who was riding by. He hid behind a tree when the witch arrived and watched as she clambered up into the tower. He longed to meet the girl with the lovely voice and so when the witch had gone, he climbed up Rapunzel's plaits and jumped inside the room.

Rapunzel was astonished to see this handsome stranger kneeling before her but he spoke to her gently.

"Have no fear," he said. "You have won my heart with your beautiful singing and now my happiness would be complete if you would agree to become my bride."

Rapunzel did not need to think twice and soon they they had planned her escape.

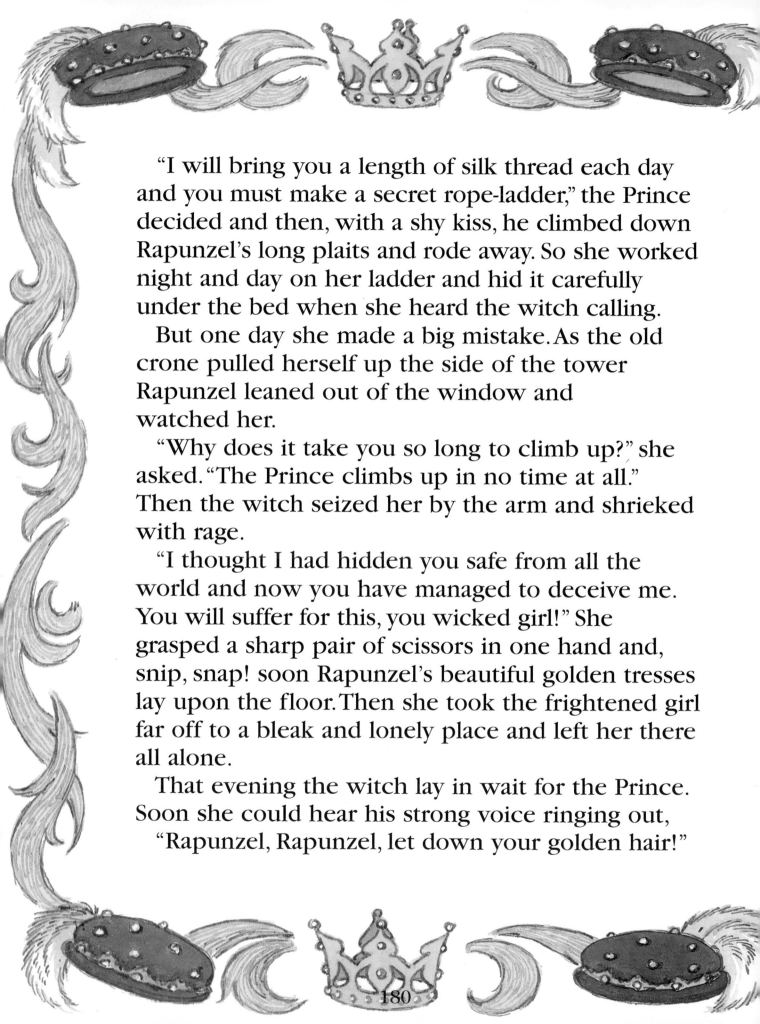

"I will bring you a length of silk thread each day and you must make a secret rope-ladder," the Prince decided and then, with a shy kiss, he climbed down Rapunzel's long plaits and rode away. So she worked night and day on her ladder and hid it carefully under the bed when she heard the witch calling.

But one day she made a big mistake. As the old crone pulled herself up the side of the tower Rapunzel leaned out of the window and watched her.

"Why does it take you so long to climb up?" she asked. "The Prince climbs up in no time at all." Then the witch seized her by the arm and shrieked with rage.

"I thought I had hidden you safe from all the world and now you have managed to deceive me. You will suffer for this, you wicked girl!" She grasped a sharp pair of scissors in one hand and, snip, snap! soon Rapunzel's beautiful golden tresses lay upon the floor. Then she took the frightened girl far off to a bleak and lonely place and left her there all alone.

That evening the witch lay in wait for the Prince. Soon she could hear his strong voice ringing out,

"Rapunzel, Rapunzel, let down your golden hair!"

The witch tied Rapunzel's plaits to a hook on the wall and threw them out of the window. In a trice the Prince had scrambled up and leapt inside, but what a shock he got to find not his beloved Rapunzel but the horrible witch awaiting him!

"Ha, ha, ha!" she cackled. "Your little bird has flown! I have hidden Rapunzel far, far away and you will never see her pretty face again."

The Prince was filled with despair and the sight of the evil witch so revolted him that he jumped right out of the window. He landed in the rose bushes that grew around the foot of the tower and their sharp thorns pierced his eyes. He was blinded and, hardly knowing what he was doing, he wandered off through the forest in search of his sweet love.

The birds and beasts brought him food to eat and without their nuts and berries he would surely have starved to death. The animals listened sorrowfully as he wept for the loss of his lovely bride but they did not know where she was hidden and they could not help.

So the Prince strayed through the wilderness for many weeks and with each step his heart grew heavier and heavier.

The little birds tried to lift his low spirits by singing to him, but their song could not compare to that wonderful voice he had heard so long ago in the tall tower. The months passed by until one day a new birdsong was carried to him on the faint breeze and his heart stopped still.

He had heard that song once before. Could it be his Rapunzel? He stumbled blindly towards the sound and although he could not see her, Rapunzel looked up and saw her Prince at once. She ran into his arms and held him close. As she wept for joy two of her tears dropped on his eyes and suddenly they grew clear and he could see as well as ever.

"You will never be parted from me again," he promised Rapunzel, and so they made their way to his kingdom and there they were married. They heard no more from the wicked witch and Rapunzel and her Prince lived happily ever after.

Just So Stories

The *Just So* stories by Rudyard Kipling (1865-1936) have delighted children for generations with their far-fetched explanations of how animals came to acquire their peculiar characteristics. Kipling may well have got the idea from the Uncle Remus stories of Joel Chandler Harris, such as *Why Mr Possum has no Hair upon his Tail*.

Illustrated by Jo Caine

THE ELEPHANT'S CHILD

In the High and Far-Off Times the Elephant, O Best Beloved, had no trunk. He had only a blackish, bulgy nose, as big as a boot, that he could wriggle about from side to side, but he couldn't pick up things with it. Now there was one Elephant, a new Elephant, an Elephant's Child, who was full of 'satiable curtiosity — and that means he asked ever so many questions. *And* he lived in Africa and he filled all Africa with his 'satiable curtiosities.

He asked his tall aunt, the Ostrich, why her tail-feathers grew just so. He asked his tall uncle, the Giraffe, what made his skin spotty. He asked his broad aunt, the Hippopotamus, why her eyes were red and he asked his hairy uncle, the Baboon, why melons tasted just so. He asked questions about everything that he saw, or heard, or felt, or smelt, or touched, and his aunts and his uncles spanked and spanked him but *still* he was full of 'satiable curtiosity!

One fine morning the Elephant's Child asked a new fine question that he had never asked before.

"What does the Crocodile have for dinner?" he said. Then everybody said "Hush!" and spanked him well.

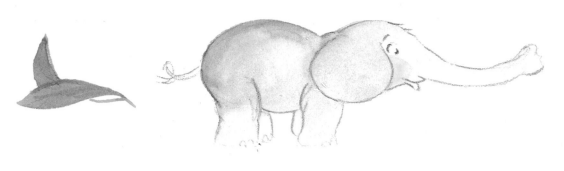

When they had quite finished, the Elephant's Child
came upon Kolokolo Bird sitting in a thorn bush.
   "If you want to find out what the Crocodile has
for dinner," said the Bird, "you must go to the banks
of the great gray-green, greasy Limpopo River, all set
about with fever-trees, and there you will find out."
So the Elephant's Child set off to find the Crocodile.
Now you must understand, O Best Beloved, that this
'satiable Elephant's Child had never seen a
Crocodile, and did not know what one was like.

190

But nevertheless he set off for the Limpopo River and the first thing that he found was a Bi-Colored-Python-Rock-Snake curled round a rock.

"'Scuse me," said the Elephant's Child most politely, "but have you seen such a thing as a Crocodile in these promiscuous parts?"

Then the Bi-Colored-Python-Rock-Snake uncoiled himself very quickly from the rock, and spanked the Elephant's Child with his scalesome, flailsome tail, and when he had finished the Elephant's Child thanked him politely and continued on his way.

After a while he trod on what he thought was a log of wood at the very edge of the great gray-green, greasy Limpopo River, but it was really the Crocodile, O Best Beloved, and the Crocodile winked one eye — like this!

"'Scuse me," said the Elephant's Child most politely, "but do you happen to have seen a Crocodile in these promiscuous parts?"

Then the Crocodile winked the other eye, and lifted half his tail out of the mud, and the Elephant's Child stepped back most politely, because he did not wish to be spanked again.

"Come hither, Little One," said the Crocodile. "Why do you ask me such things?"

"'Scuse me," said the Elephant's Child, "but all my aunts and uncles have spanked me and the Bi-Coloured-Python-Rock-Snake has spanked me and so, if it's all the same to you, I don't want to be spanked again."

"Come hither, Little One," said the Crocodile, "for I am the Crocodile," and he wept crocodile tears to show it was quite true. Then the Elephant's Child grew all breathless, and panted, and then he spoke.

"You are the very person I have been looking for all these long days. Will you please tell me what you have for dinner?"

"Come hither, Little One," said the Crocodile, "and I'll whisper."

Then the Elephant's Child put his head down close to the Crocodile's musky, tusky mouth, and the Crocodile caught him by his little nose, which up to that moment had been no bigger than a boot.

"I think," said the Crocodile from between his teeth, like this, "I think today I will begin with Elephant's Child!" and he pulled and he pulled and he pulled.

"Led go!" said the Elephant's Child. "You are hurtig me!" Then the Bi-Colored-Python-Rock-Snake scuffled down the bank and knotted himself in a double-clove-hitch around the Elephant's Child's legs.

And he pulled, and the Elephant's Child pulled, and the Crocodile pulled — but the Elephant's Child and the Bi-Colored-Python-Rock-Snake pulled hardest (and by this time the poor nose was nearly five feet long!)

At last the Crocodile let go of the Elephant's Child's nose with a plop that you could hear all up and down the Limpopo. Then the Elephant's child dangled his poor pulled nose in the water.

"I am waiting for it to shrink," he explained.

There he sat for three days patiently waiting for his nose to shrink back to its usual size but the long stretched nose never grew any shorter. For, O Best Beloved, you will see and understand that the Crocodile had pulled it out into a really truly trunk same as all Elephants have today.

At the end of the third day a fly came and stung him on the shoulder and before he knew what he was doing he lifted up his trunk and hit that fly dead with the end of it. Later he grew hungry, so almost without thinking he put out his trunk and plucked a large bundle of grass and stuffed it in his mouth.

"The sun is very hot here," said the Elephant's Child, and before he thought what he was doing he schlooped up a schloop of mud from the banks of the river and he slapped it on his head where it made a cool schloopy-sloshy mud cap all trickly behind his ears.

Then the Elephant's Child went home across Africa and how proud he was of his useful new nose. And the first thing he did when he saw all his relations was to spank them with his long trunk — and after that, none of them dared spank anyone ever again!

THE CAT THAT WALKED BY HIMSELF

Hear and attend; for this befell and behappened, O Best Beloved, when the Tame animals were wild. The Dog was wild, and the Horse was wild, and the Cow was wild, and the Sheep was wild, and the Pig was wild — as wild as wild could be — and they all walked in the Wet Wild Woods by their wild lones.

But the wildest of all the wild animals was the Cat. He walked by himself and all places were alike to him.

Of course the Man was wild too. He was dreadfully wild. He didn't even begin to be tame till he met the Woman, and she told him that she did not like living in his wild ways.

So she found a nice dry cave to lie down in and she lit a nice fire of wood at the back of the cave. Then she hung a dried wild-horse skin across the opening of the cave, and she said, "Wipe your feet, dear, when you come in, and now we'll keep house."

That night as the Man slept by the fire, the Woman sat up combing her hair. She took the bone of a shoulder of mutton and she looked at the wonderful marks that were carved on it and she made the First Singing Magic in the world. Out in the Wet Wild Woods the wild animals could see the bright light of the fire and they wondered what it meant.

Wild Dog lifted up his head and said, "I will go up and see and look. Cat, come with me."

"Nenni!" said the Cat. "I am the Cat who walks by himself, and all places are alike to me. I will not come." But after Wild Dog had set off, the Cat secretly followed him and hid himself where he could see everything.

Wild Dog entered the cave and sniffed the beautiful smell of the roast mutton and the Woman laughed.

"Here comes the first Wild Thing out of the Wild Woods, what do you want?"

Wild Dog said, "O my Enemy and Wife of my Enemy, what is this that smells so good in the Wild Woods?" Then the Woman gave him the bone to gnaw and it was so delicious that he wanted another.

"Wild Thing out of the Wild Woods," said the Woman. "Help my Man to hunt through the day and guard this cave at night, and I will give you as many bones as you need." And so the Wild Dog became the First Friend.

"Ah!" said the Cat, listening. "This is a very wise Woman, but she is not so wise as I am."

The next night the Woman made a Second Magic and this time the Wild Horse went to see the strange light.

The Cat followed very softly and watched him enter the cave. The Woman laughed and said, "Here comes the second Wild Thing out of the Wild Woods, what do you want?" Then the Wild Horse looked at the sweet grass that lay in a mound on the floor of the cave.

"Bend your head and wear this halter," said the Woman, "and you shall eat the grass three times a day."

"Ah!" said the Cat. "This is a clever Woman, but she is not so clever as I am."

When the Man and the Dog came back from hunting, the Man said, "What is Wild Horse doing here?"

And the Woman said, "He is now the First Servant and he will carry us from place to place for always."

The next day the Woman made her Third Magic and this time the Wild Cow came up to the cave and she promised to give her milk to the Woman every day in return for the wonderful grass. The Cat went back through the Wet Wild Woods and he never told anybody what he had seen.

But in the morning he went back to the cave and he saw the light of the fire and he smelt the warm milk. Then the Woman laughed and said, "Wild Thing out of the Wild Woods, go away for I have put away the magic bone, and we have no more need of either friends or servants in our cave."

Cat said, "I am not a friend, and I am not a servant. I am the Cat who walks by himself, and I wish to come in."

"No," said the Woman. "If you are the Cat who walks by himself, all places are alike to you. Go away and walk by yourself in all places alike." But the Cat liked the warm cave and he spoke again.

"You are very wise and beautiful," he said. "You should not be cruel, even to a Cat." Then the Woman laughed.

"I knew I was wise, but I did not know I was beautiful. So I will make a bargain with you. If ever I say one word in your praise, you may come into the cave. And if ever I say two words in your praise, you may sit by the fire. And if ever I say three words in your praise, you may drink the warm milk for always and always."

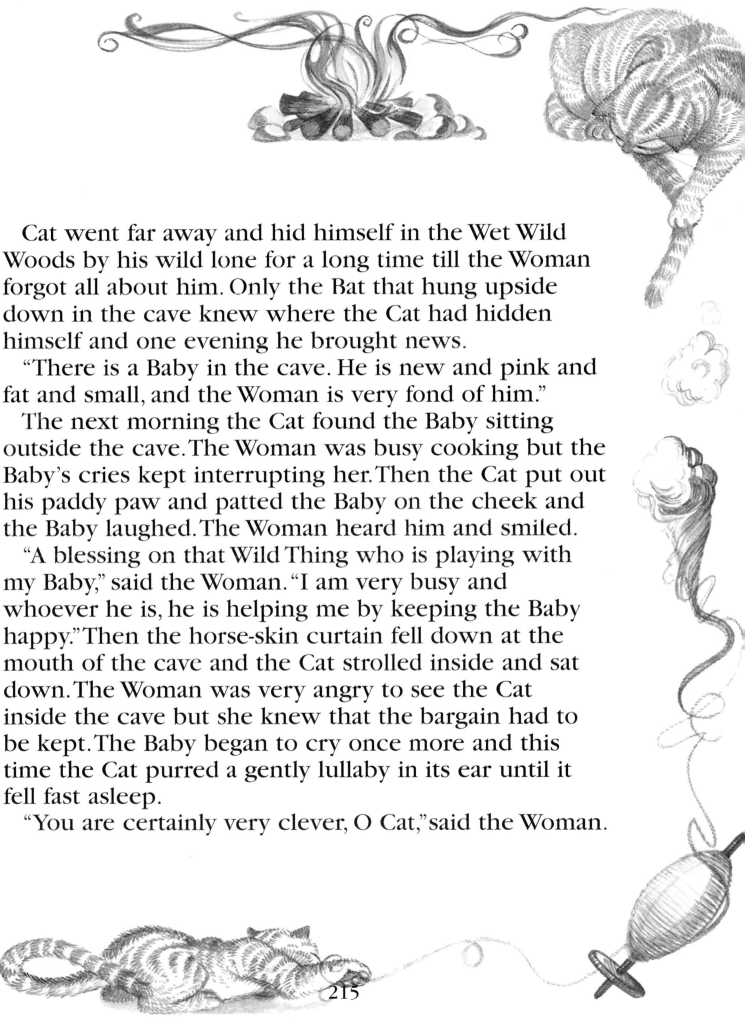

Cat went far away and hid himself in the Wet Wild Woods by his wild lone for a long time till the Woman forgot all about him. Only the Bat that hung upside down in the cave knew where the Cat had hidden himself and one evening he brought news.

"There is a Baby in the cave. He is new and pink and fat and small, and the Woman is very fond of him."

The next morning the Cat found the Baby sitting outside the cave. The Woman was busy cooking but the Baby's cries kept interrupting her. Then the Cat put out his paddy paw and patted the Baby on the cheek and the Baby laughed. The Woman heard him and smiled.

"A blessing on that Wild Thing who is playing with my Baby," said the Woman. "I am very busy and whoever he is, he is helping me by keeping the Baby happy." Then the horse-skin curtain fell down at the mouth of the cave and the Cat strolled inside and sat down. The Woman was very angry to see the Cat inside the cave but she knew that the bargain had to be kept. The Baby began to cry once more and this time the Cat purred a gently lullaby in its ear until it fell fast asleep.

"You are certainly very clever, O Cat," said the Woman.

Then the smoke suddenly puffed up from the fire and when it had cleared, there was the Cat sitting quite comfy close to the heat of the flames.

"Now I can sit by the warm fire for always and always," said the Cat, "but still I am the Cat who walks by himself, and all places are alike to me." But the Woman was very angry and promised herself she would not say a third word in praise of the Cat.

By and by the cave grew so still that a little mouse crept out of a corner and ran across the floor.

"Ouh! Chee!" cried the Woman, and she jumped upon a stool. Then the Cat made one pounce and caught the little mouse in his claws.

"A hundred thanks," said the Woman. "You must be very wise to catch a mouse so easily."

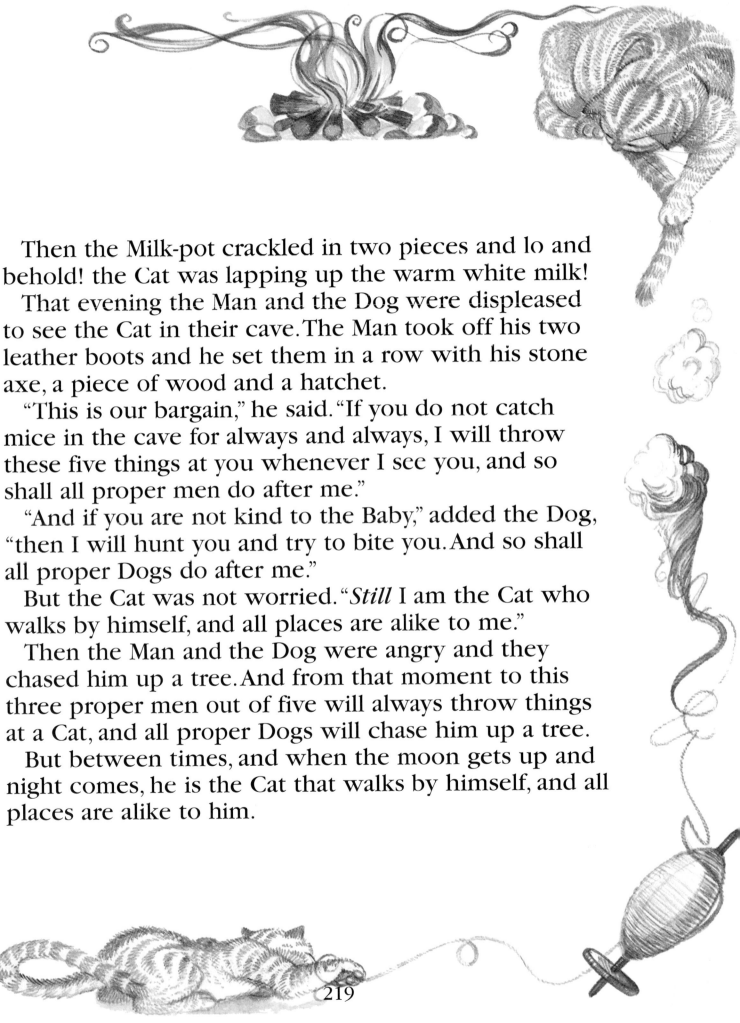

Then the Milk-pot crackled in two pieces and lo and behold! the Cat was lapping up the warm white milk!

That evening the Man and the Dog were displeased to see the Cat in their cave. The Man took off his two leather boots and he set them in a row with his stone axe, a piece of wood and a hatchet.

"This is our bargain," he said. "If you do not catch mice in the cave for always and always, I will throw these five things at you whenever I see you, and so shall all proper men do after me."

"And if you are not kind to the Baby," added the Dog, "then I will hunt you and try to bite you. And so shall all proper Dogs do after me."

But the Cat was not worried. "*Still* I am the Cat who walks by himself, and all places are alike to me."

Then the Man and the Dog were angry and they chased him up a tree. And from that moment to this three proper men out of five will always throw things at a Cat, and all proper Dogs will chase him up a tree.

But between times, and when the moon gets up and night comes, he is the Cat that walks by himself, and all places are alike to him.

HOW THE CAMEL GOT HIS HUMP

Now this tale tells how the Camel got his big hump. In the beginning of years, when the world was so new-and-all, and the Animals were just beginning to work for Man, there lived a Camel, and he lived in the middle of a Howling Desert because he did not want to work.

He ate thorns and tamarisks and milkweed and prickles and was most 'scruciating idle, and when anybody spoke to him he said "Humph!" Just "Humph!" and no more. The Dog and the Horse and the Ox each tried to persuade him to help them with the work but the Camel would only reply "Humph!" Now the other animals thought that this was most unfair so when one day the Djinn of All Deserts came rolling along in a cloud of dust (Djinns always travel that way because it is Magic), they asked for help.

"Djinn of All Deserts," said the Horse, "is it right for any one to be idle, with the world so new-and-all? There is a thing in the middle of your Howling Desert with a long neck and long legs and he won't do a stroke of work."

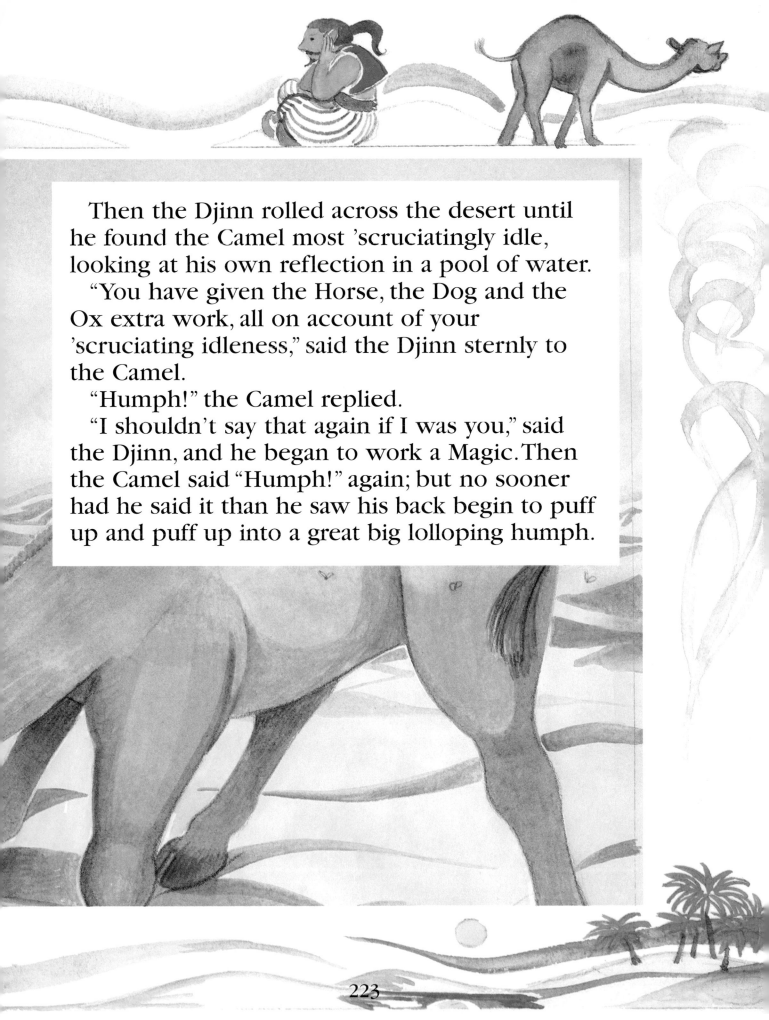

Then the Djinn rolled across the desert until he found the Camel most 'scruciatingly idle, looking at his own reflection in a pool of water.

"You have given the Horse, the Dog and the Ox extra work, all on account of your 'scruciating idleness," said the Djinn sternly to the Camel.

"Humph!" the Camel replied.

"I shouldn't say that again if I was you," said the Djinn, and he began to work a Magic. Then the Camel said "Humph!" again; but no sooner had he said it than he saw his back begin to puff up and puff up into a great big lolloping humph.

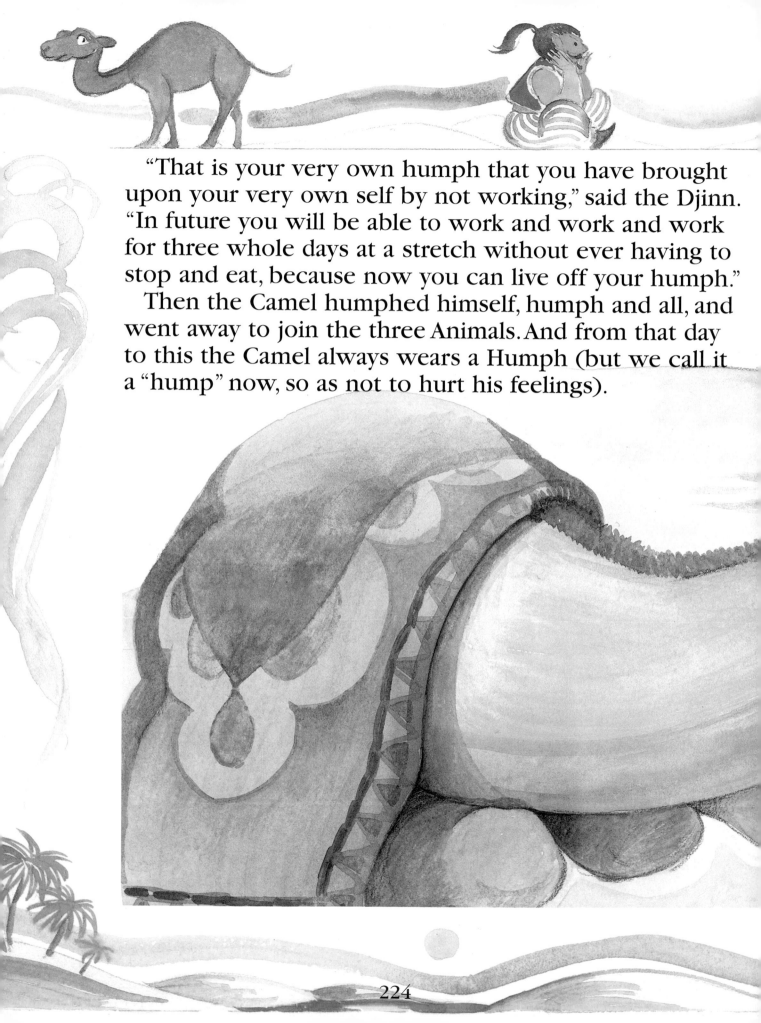

"That is your very own humph that you have brought upon your very own self by not working," said the Djinn. "In future you will be able to work and work and work for three whole days at a stretch without ever having to stop and eat, because now you can live off your humph."

Then the Camel humphed himself, humph and all, and went away to join the three Animals. And from that day to this the Camel always wears a Humph (but we call it a "hump" now, so as not to hurt his feelings).

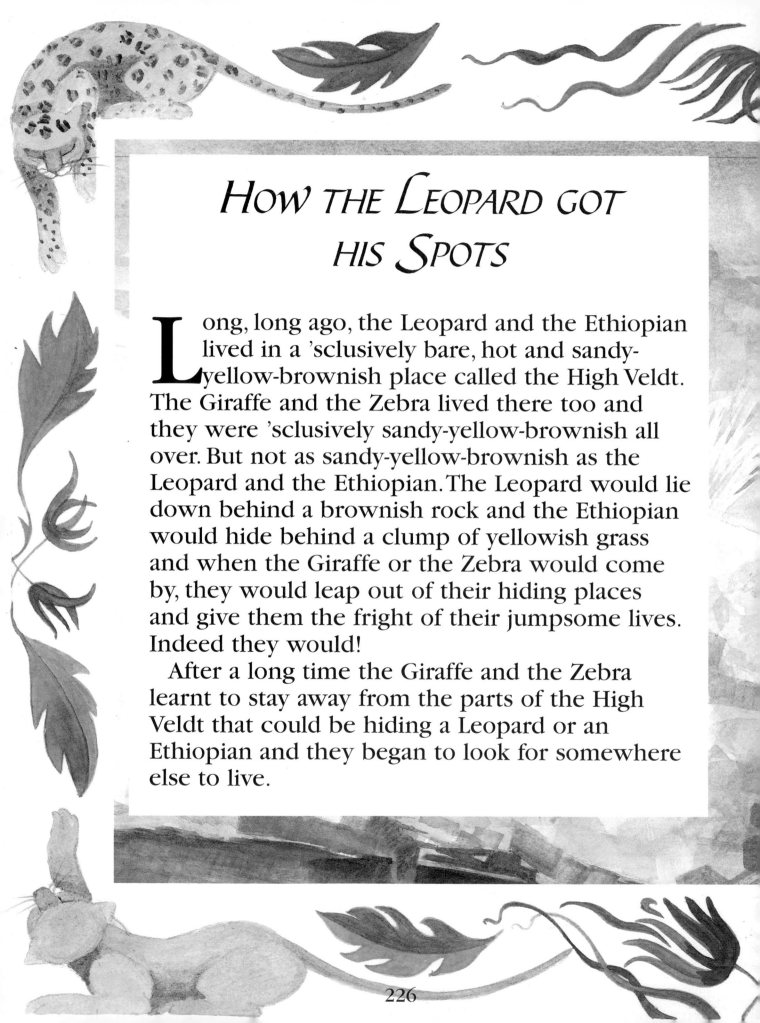

How the Leopard got his Spots

Long, long ago, the Leopard and the Ethiopian lived in a 'sclusively bare, hot and sandy-yellow-brownish place called the High Veldt. The Giraffe and the Zebra lived there too and they were 'sclusively sandy-yellow-brownish all over. But not as sandy-yellow-brownish as the Leopard and the Ethiopian. The Leopard would lie down behind a brownish rock and the Ethiopian would hide behind a clump of yellowish grass and when the Giraffe or the Zebra would come by, they would leap out of their hiding places and give them the fright of their jumpsome lives. Indeed they would!

After a long time the Giraffe and the Zebra learnt to stay away from the parts of the High Veldt that could be hiding a Leopard or an Ethiopian and they began to look for somewhere else to live.

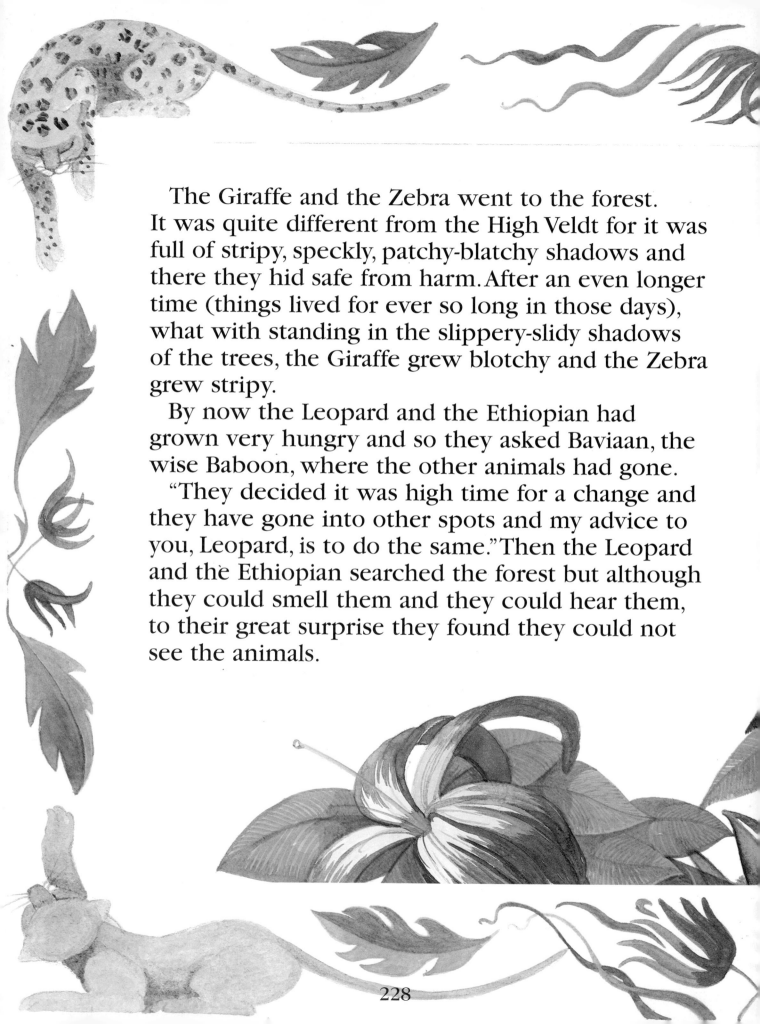

The Giraffe and the Zebra went to the forest. It was quite different from the High Veldt for it was full of stripy, speckly, patchy-blatchy shadows and there they hid safe from harm. After an even longer time (things lived for ever so long in those days), what with standing in the slippery-slidy shadows of the trees, the Giraffe grew blotchy and the Zebra grew stripy.

By now the Leopard and the Ethiopian had grown very hungry and so they asked Baviaan, the wise Baboon, where the other animals had gone.

"They decided it was high time for a change and they have gone into other spots and my advice to you, Leopard, is to do the same." Then the Leopard and the Ethiopian searched the forest but although they could smell them and they could hear them, to their great surprise they found they could not see the animals.

Soon it grew dark, and then the Leopard heard something breathing sniffily quite near him. It smelt like Zebra and when he stretched out his paw it felt like Zebra. So the Leopard jumped out of his tree and sat on this strange thing until morning because there was something about it that he didn't quite like.

Presently he heard a grunt and a crash and he heard the Ethiopian call out.

"I've caught a thing that I cannot see. It smells like Giraffe and it kicks like Giraffe but it hasn't any shape."

"Don't trust it," advised the Leopard. "Just sit on its head till the morning comes, same as me." So there they sat and waited until the sun rose for then the light would show them just what they had caught.

At sunrise the Leopard looked over at the Ethiopian.

"What have you got down your end of the table, Brother?" he asked. The Ethiopian scratched his head.

"Well, it ought to be Giraffe, but it is covered all over with chestnut blotches. What have you got?"

"Well, it ought to be Zebra," replied the Leopard, equally puzzled, "but it's covered all over with black stripes. What have you both been doing to yourselves?"

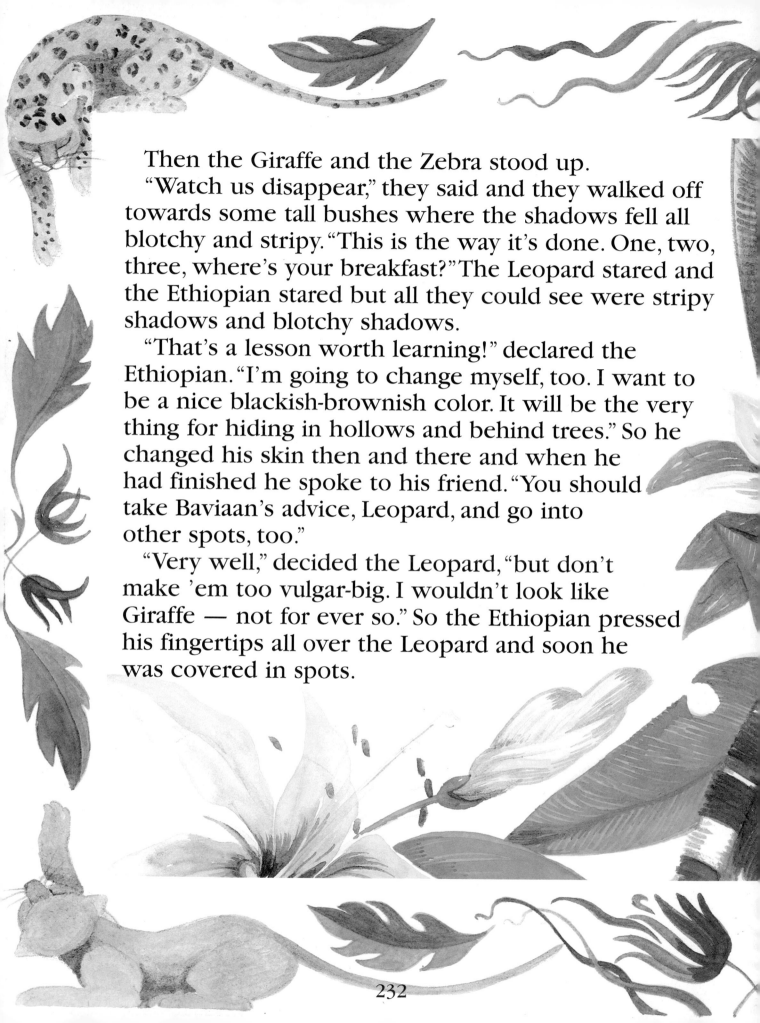

Then the Giraffe and the Zebra stood up.

"Watch us disappear," they said and they walked off towards some tall bushes where the shadows fell all blotchy and stripy. "This is the way it's done. One, two, three, where's your breakfast?" The Leopard stared and the Ethiopian stared but all they could see were stripy shadows and blotchy shadows.

"That's a lesson worth learning!" declared the Ethiopian. "I'm going to change myself, too. I want to be a nice blackish-brownish color. It will be the very thing for hiding in hollows and behind trees." So he changed his skin then and there and when he had finished he spoke to his friend. "You should take Baviaan's advice, Leopard, and go into other spots, too."

"Very well," decided the Leopard, "but don't make 'em too vulgar-big. I wouldn't look like Giraffe — not for ever so." So the Ethiopian pressed his fingertips all over the Leopard and soon he was covered in spots.

Wherever the Ethiopian's five fingers touched his coat, they left five little black marks, all close together. Sometimes his fingers slipped and the marks got a little blurred, but if you look closely at any Leopard now you will see that there are always five spots — off five fat black fingertips.

"Now you can lie out on the ground and look like a heap of pebbles," said the Ethiopian. "You can lie on a leafy branch and look like dappled sunshine. Think of that and purr!"

And so the animals were very proud of their new coats and were very glad that they had changed. Oh, one last thing. Now and again you will hear grown-ups say, "Can the Leopard change his spots?" I don't think even grown-ups would keep on saying such a silly thing if the Leopard hadn't done it once — do you? But they will never do it again, Best Beloved. Oh no, they are quite contented just as they are.

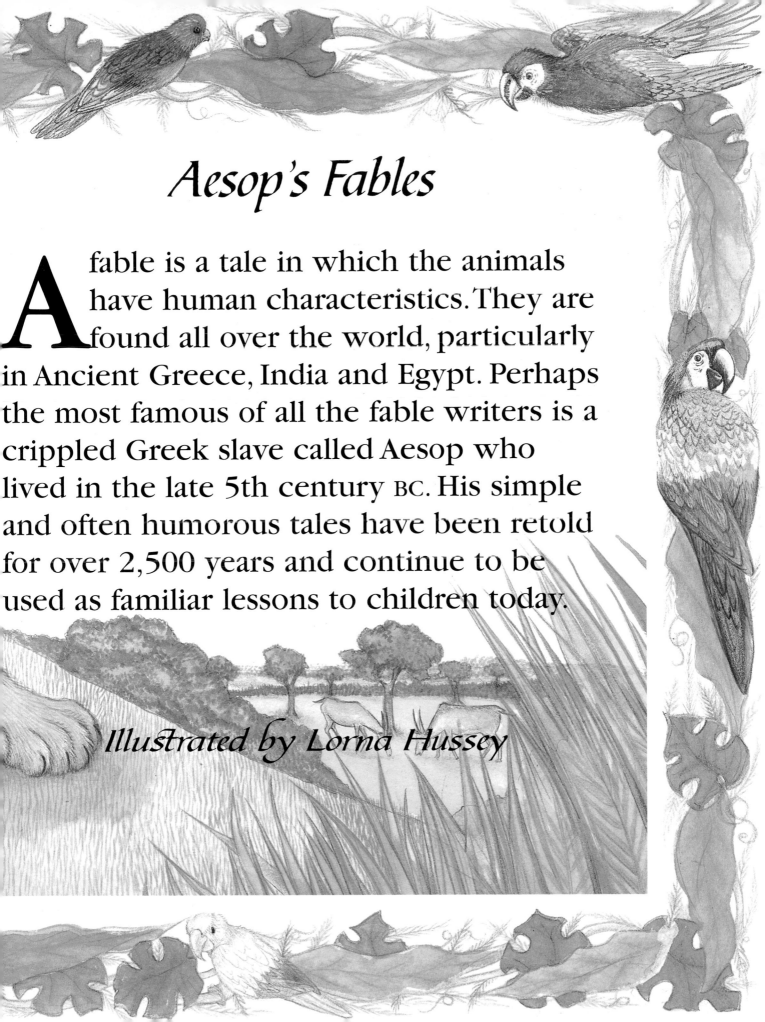

Aesop's Fables

A fable is a tale in which the animals have human characteristics. They are found all over the world, particularly in Ancient Greece, India and Egypt. Perhaps the most famous of all the fable writers is a crippled Greek slave called Aesop who lived in the late 5th century BC. His simple and often humorous tales have been retold for over 2,500 years and continue to be used as familiar lessons to children today.

Illustrated by Lorna Hussey

The Wolf and the Ass

O ne day the Ass set off to find some sweet grass to eat. He followed the path from the jungle and soon found himself far away from his usual haunts. Here the grass was lush and green and soon the Ass was busy chewing away, quite contented and without a care in the world.

But as he munched happily in the meadow a big gray Wolf crept up on him unawares. Suddenly the Ass pricked up his ears for he could hear the pad of soft paws behind him.

"That Wolf means to make me his supper!" said the Donkey to himself.

When the Wolf was close enough to pounce, the Ass lifted his head and called out quite calmly.

"I shouldn't do that if I was you," he said. The Wolf was astonished. Why was the Ass so unafraid?

"I have trodden on a sharp thorn," explained the Ass, "and if you eat me it will be sure to stick in your throat. I am sure you wouldn't want that."

The Wolf shook his head and the Ass continued.

"I will lift up my hoof and then you can pull out the thorn before you eat me," he offered helpfully. The Wolf could not believe his luck. He stood behind the Ass and as the Ass waited patiently with his hoof in the air, the Wolf had a good look for the thorn. But there was no thorn to be found.

Then the Ass summoned up all his strength and with a loud and triumphant whinny he gave a mighty kick. The Wolf flew head over heels into the air and landed in the middle of a thorn bush, howling with pain.

"That Ass is not as stupid as he looks," thought the Wolf to himself as he picked the thorns from his bottom, one by one, but the Ass just smiled at him sweetly as he trotted off home.

AND THE MORAL OF THIS STORY IS:
BEWARE OF UNEXPECTED FAVORS

The Dog and his Reflection

There was once a naughty Dog. He loved to sit outside the Butcher's shop and admire the strings of shiny sausages and rows of pink pork chops. How he wished he could help himself to something to eat!

One day when the Butcher's back was turned, the Dog ran into the shop and seized a large ham bone in his strong teeth. Off down the street he ran while the Butcher waved his sharpest knife and shouted after him angrily.

"Nobody has a bone as big and as tasty as mine!" the Dog said to himself as he set off for home. But as he crossed the bridge what should he see but another Dog with another bone — and this bone was just as big as his own! The Dog was astonished.

"I shall have that bone," he decided. "Two bones are better than one!" With that, the silly Dog opened his mouth and snapped greedily.

But what a shock he got when his own bone tumbled from his mouth and landed with a splash in the water. To the Dog's great dismay the bone sank quickly out of sight and he realized he was left with nothing at all.

Slowly he trudged back to his kennel, feeling very sorry for himself. He lay down and rested his head upon his paws. What a tragedy it was to have something in your grasp and then have it snatched suddenly away.

"I was wrong," sighed the Dog unhappily. "One bone is much, much better than none."

AND THE MORAL OF THIS STORY IS:
BE GRATEFUL FOR WHAT YOU HAVE

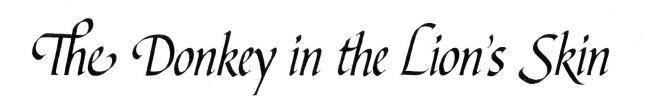

The Donkey in the Lion's Skin

There was once an unhappy Donkey. He lived in the jungle with all the other animals but they were cruel and often made fun of him. How he wished he could get his own back on the unfriendly creatures but whenever they saw him they just laughed and called him rude names.

One day the Donkey had quite a fright. As he trotted along the jungle path he thought he saw a Lion waiting to pounce on him. But the Lion didn't move and then the Donkey realised that it was not a real Lion after all, but just a Lion's skin.

"This would make a fine costume for me to wear," said the Donkey and he slipped it over his back. He looked exactly like a real Lion!

"Now I can teach those animals a lesson," said the Donkey, and he hid in a thicket and waited for someone to pass by. Soon the Monkey came swinging along, clinging to the vines with his tail. Out jumped the Donkey with a fierce roar and the Monkey ran screeching up a tree. Then the Bear came ambling along the path but when he saw the Lion he ran whimpering into the bushes.

Then the fierce Tiger came prowling by but when the Donkey jumped out at him, he ran off into the jungle as fast as he could. The happy Donkey had never had so much fun in all his life! He stamped his hooves with glee and rocked with silent laughter.

The sun was slowly sinking in the west as the crafty Fox slunk into view. With his head bent low, he sniffed for food amongst the shrubs and grasses. He could smell all sorts of interesting things, but he could not smell danger so imagine his surprise when out rushed the Donkey in the Lion's skin! To the Donkey's great delight the terrified Fox yelped and ran for cover with his tail between his legs.

But this time the silly Donkey could not help himself and he laughed out loud. His loud bray echoed through the jungle and the wily Fox stood stock still. Slowly he walked back to the fierce Lion skin and looked under the great head. There he came face to face with the embarrassed Donkey and the silly animal hung his head low.

The Fox laughed long and loud and then all the other animals came running.

The astonished creatures gathered around the blushing Donkey and soon the jungle rang to the sounds of their catcalls and hoots of glee.

"Why, it wasn't a fierce Lion who pounced out on me after all!" cried the Monkey. "It was just the silly old Donkey," grumbled the Bear.

The Donkey looked very ashamed.

"You foolish Donkey!" said the Fox. "If only you had kept your mouth shut, your trick might well have succeeded but you just had to give your game away with your loud bray!"

AND THE MORAL OF THIS STORY IS:
A FOOL MAY DECEIVE OTHERS WITH HIS
APPEARANCE BUT HIS WORDS WILL SOON REVEAL HIM

The Lion and the Mouse

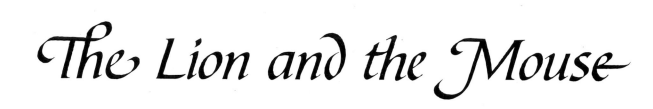

There was once a mighty Lion. He was powerful and strong and when he roared, the earth shook, the parrots squawked and the monkeys ran chattering to the treetops.

All the animals were afraid of him and they called him the King of the Beasts. The little Mouse was especially frightened of the Lion for she knew that if one of his paws landed on top of her, she would be squashed as flat as a blade of grass. She tried her best to keep well away from the King of the Beasts.

One day, as the Lion slept in the shade of an old acacia tree, the Mouse was scuttling busily about her business, searching for small seeds to eat. Little did she know that her scurrying steps took her close by the sleeping Lion. Up his leg she scampered, all the time thinking he was nothing but a smooth termite hill. But as her feet ran tickling across his back the Lion awoke with a mighty roar. The little mouse tumbled to the ground and in a flash he had trapped her tail under one enormous paw.

"What is the meaning of this?" he rumbled and the Mouse shook with fright. "Do you not know who I am?"

The little Mouse could feel his hot breath singeing her whiskers and she nodded her head up and down rapidly.

"Yes, yes!" she gasped. "You are the King of the Beasts, the Lord of the Jungle, the mighty Lion."

"That is so," smiled the Lion approvingly. "Just so," and he tightened his grip on her tail.

"Oh, please have pity on me," the Mouse begged. "If you save my life today why, who knows, perhaps one day I shall save yours."

The Lion threw back his head and laughed and laughed. "*You* save *my* life?" he said. "A little Mouse save the King of the Beasts? That I should certainly like to see."

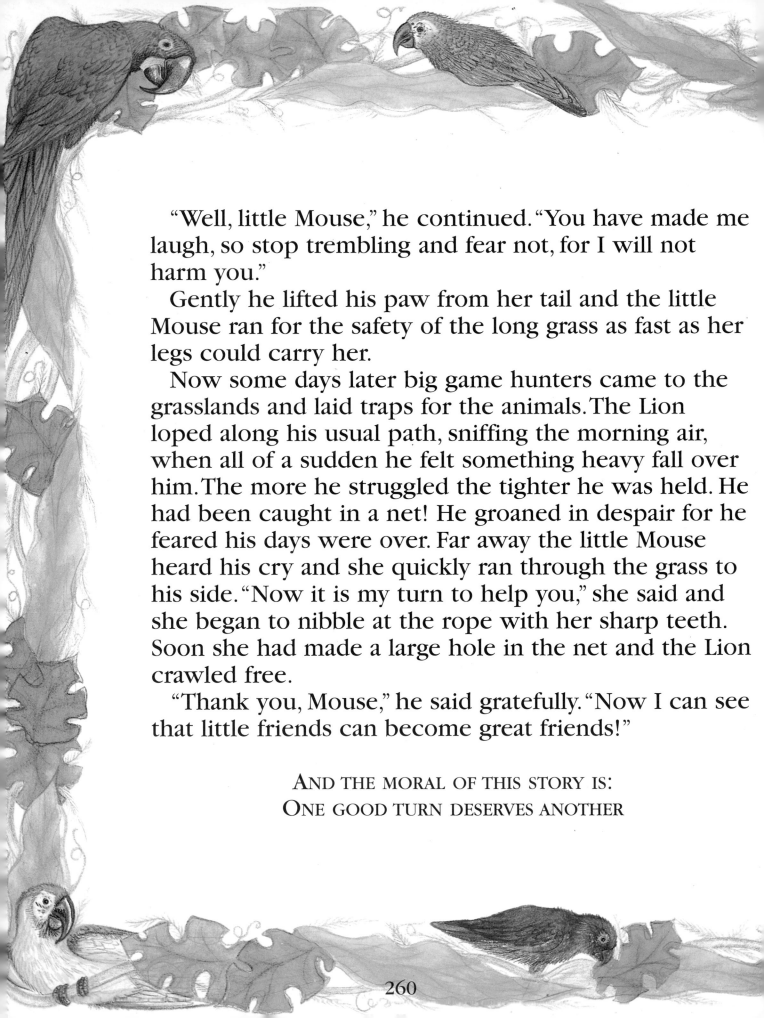

"Well, little Mouse," he continued. "You have made me laugh, so stop trembling and fear not, for I will not harm you."

Gently he lifted his paw from her tail and the little Mouse ran for the safety of the long grass as fast as her legs could carry her.

Now some days later big game hunters came to the grasslands and laid traps for the animals. The Lion loped along his usual path, sniffing the morning air, when all of a sudden he felt something heavy fall over him. The more he struggled the tighter he was held. He had been caught in a net! He groaned in despair for he feared his days were over. Far away the little Mouse heard his cry and she quickly ran through the grass to his side. "Now it is my turn to help you," she said and she began to nibble at the rope with her sharp teeth. Soon she had made a large hole in the net and the Lion crawled free.

"Thank you, Mouse," he said gratefully. "Now I can see that little friends can become great friends!"

AND THE MORAL OF THIS STORY IS:
ONE GOOD TURN DESERVES ANOTHER

The Fox and the Stork

One day a Fox decided to invite a Stork to tea. He made all the preparations in the kitchen and set the table with his best crockery. He brushed his fine long tail until it shone like copper and then dressed in his best blue coat.

Soon there was a tap, tap, tap upon the door. It was the Stork and with a great flourish, the Fox opened the door and bowed low.

"Do step inside," he cried. "Welcome to my humble home." The Stork looked very elegant in a beautiful purple hat and matching cape and as she stepped daintily into the room her hat feathers quivered. She was very hungry. "I do hope the Fox has plenty of food," she said to herself anxiously.

"I have cooked some beautiful soup," announced the Fox. "Let us begin." And he showed the Stork to a chair. But the poor Stork was dismayed to see that the only plates laid upon the table were quite flat. How would she be able to eat off such a dish?

The Fox came bustling in from the kitchen and carefully set a steaming pot of soup down in the center of the table.

The Fox ladled out the soup with much smacking of lips and many appreciative sniffs. Then he sat down, lifted his spoon and smiled broadly at the Stork.

"Do tuck in!" he urged. "This is my best soup!"

But the Stork looked down at her plate and sighed unhappily. She could not swallow this soup with her long pointed beak and so she could only sit and watch as the Fox greedily lapped up his plateful.

When the Fox had quite finished he looked across at the Stork in surprise.

"Did you not enjoy the soup?" he asked, wrinkling his brow as if greatly concerned. But the poor Stork was too polite to complain and so the wily Fox lapped up her portion as well.

The next day when the Stork awoke she was still hungry. She decided to repay the Fox's hospitality and invited him to dinner that evening. He was delighted and accepted eagerly.

But as the Fox sat down to eat at the Stork's table he could hardly believe his eyes. The only dishes upon the table were two tall jugs! The Stork dipped her slender beak inside the jug and drank her soup but the Fox could only lick his lips hungrily and watch, for there was no way he could get at the food.

He returned home a sadder and wiser Fox with nobody to blame but himself for, as he plainly realized, he had only been paid back for his own uncaring behavior.

AND THE MORAL OF THIS STORY IS:
DO AS YOU WOULD BE DONE BY

The Town Mouse and the Country Mouse

Once upon a time there were two little mice. One mouse was very grand and lived in the town but the other was quite different. He was a Country Mouse. He lived under the roots of an old oak tree in a small hole lined with straw and dry grass. He slept on a scrap of sheep's wool and wore a brown waistcoat he had made himself from an old grainsack.

"How lucky I am to live here," the Country Mouse said to himself. "I must invite my cousin to come and share my cosy home," but when the smart Town Mouse arrived, he looked about the little hole in dismay. What a shabby home! The Country Mouse laughed and led him to a table piled high with food.

"I have prepared a special meal," he said excitedly. "A cob of corn, fresh hazelnuts and rosy red rosehips."

But the Town Mouse wrinkled his nose in disgust.

"I cannot eat this food," he protested. "You must come and stay with me and discover what real food is like." So the next day the Country Mouse returned with the Town Mouse to his home in the big, busy city.

"This is what a home should be like," said the Town Mouse proudly as he led the Country Mouse from room to room. "I like soft carpets and comfortable furniture. There are no leaves or mud here."

Soon they were hungry. "Follow me," said the Town Mouse, "but there will be no rosehips or hazlenuts on the menu!" he added with a twinkle in his eye. The little Country Mouse gasped when he saw the wonderful spread laid out on the large dining table.

"This is *real* food," cried the Town Mouse. "Let us begin!" but as soon as he scampered across the floor two large dogs came bounding into the room, barking fiercely and the Country Mouse drew back in terror.

"I'm going back to my home!" he told his cousin. "You may sleep on a soft duck-down mattress under a satin quilt while I have only a scrap of wool for my bed. You may wear a red velvet coat with gold buttons while my clothes are patched and darned. You may feast on roast beef and chocolate cake while I live off the nuts and berries of the hedgerow. You can enjoy the excitement of the town if you wish but give me the plain and simple life any time!"

AND THE MORAL OF THIS STORY IS:
BETTER A POOR AND CAREFREE LIFE
THAN A RICH AND WORRIED LIFE

The Fox without a Tail

There was once a fine Fox, a most handsome fellow with a shiny red coat and a long bushy tail. This Fox was a rather vain creature and he spent long hours brushing his tail from top to tip until it shone like bright copper.

But one evening he had a most dreadful accident. As he hunted amongst the thickets and hedgerows for a tasty meal he suddenly heard a loud *clack!* and felt the most dreadful pain.

He realized at once that he had been caught in a trap and, pull as he might, his beautiful tail was stuck fast. Suddenly the pain stopped and to his great dismay the Fox found his tail lying in all its glory upon the ground. The trap had pulled it clean off. This was a calamity! Why, he was a Fox! The best and finest Fox that ever was — and what was a Fox without his tail? Why, little more than a laughing stock! How the other Foxes would taunt him when they saw him creeping by, tail-less. The very thought of it was more than he could bear.

After a while he stood up, collected his hat and made his way to the forest dell where the Foxes met for their nightly meetings. As the Fox strutted into the center of the circle a hushed silence fell on the entire company. He wore his best hat and tucked inside the hatband was his own fine red tail!

A young Fox began to titter, then another, then another, and soon the forest rang to the sounds of their rude laughter. With a dignified expression, the Fox held up his hand for silence and spoke.

"As you know, I have been blessed with a particularly fine specimen of a tail and I have been proud to carry it around behind me ever since I was born. But now I feel the time has come for a change. Tails should not drag behind us in the dirt. No, they should be worn on high, where their beauty can be fully admired."

The Fox paraded around the glade.

"This is the new fashion" he said "so you had all better start wearing your tails on your hats, like me."

Then an old Fox stood creakily to his feet.

"We have heard what you have to say, Brother Fox, but answer me this," he said. "Would you be quite so keen for us to follow this new fashion if your own tail had not been pulled off in a trap?" Then the poor Fox saw that everyone had seen through his cunning plan and he slunk off into the forest, much ashamed.

AND THE MORAL OF THIS STORY IS:
IF YOU SUFFER SOME MISFORTUNE, MAKE THE BEST OF
WHAT YOU HAVE AND DO NOT TRY TO
MAKE OTHERS SUFFER ALSO

Tales of Brer Rabbit

The *Brer Rabbit* stories began as African American fables, told by the slaves working on plantations in the deep South, and almost certainly African in origin. Joel Chandler Harris (1848-1908) turned what was often little more than a folk saying into stories full of atmosphere and fun.

ILLUSTRATED BY STEPHEN HOLMES

BRER RABBIT AND THE WELL

Brer Rabbit was hard at work in the garden with Brer Fox, Brer Raccoon and Brer Bear. The sun was hot and he was fed up.

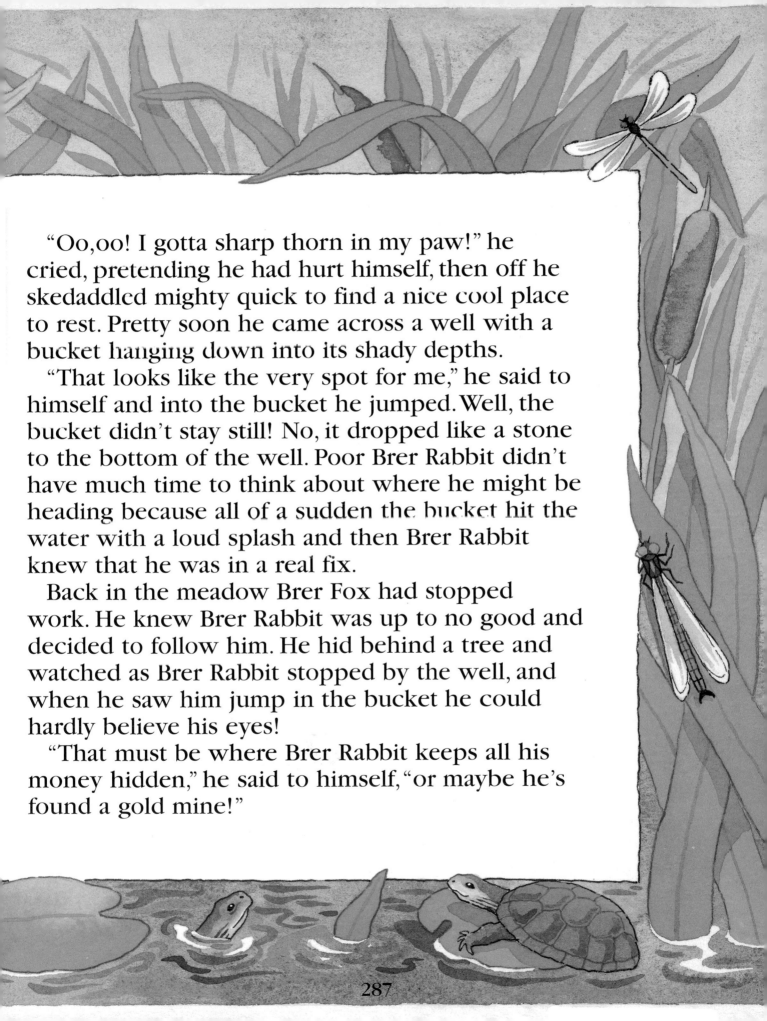

"Oo, oo! I gotta sharp thorn in my paw!" he cried, pretending he had hurt himself, then off he skedaddled mighty quick to find a nice cool place to rest. Pretty soon he came across a well with a bucket hanging down into its shady depths.

"That looks like the very spot for me," he said to himself and into the bucket he jumped. Well, the bucket didn't stay still! No, it dropped like a stone to the bottom of the well. Poor Brer Rabbit didn't have much time to think about where he might be heading because all of a sudden the bucket hit the water with a loud splash and then Brer Rabbit knew that he was in a real fix.

Back in the meadow Brer Fox had stopped work. He knew Brer Rabbit was up to no good and decided to follow him. He hid behind a tree and watched as Brer Rabbit stopped by the well, and when he saw him jump in the bucket he could hardly believe his eyes!

"That must be where Brer Rabbit keeps all his money hidden," he said to himself, "or maybe he's found a gold mine!"

Slowly he crept to the well and peered over the edge. There wasn't a sound to be heard. Down at the bottom of the well poor Brer Rabbit sat hunched up in his bucket, hardly daring to twitch a whisker. Suddenly a loud voice echoed down the well.

"Howdy, Brer Rabbit," called Brer Fox. "What are you doing down there?" Brer Rabbit thought hard.

"I'm fishing," he replied. "There are some mighty fine fish down here, Brer Fox. Why don't you come and get some for yourself?"

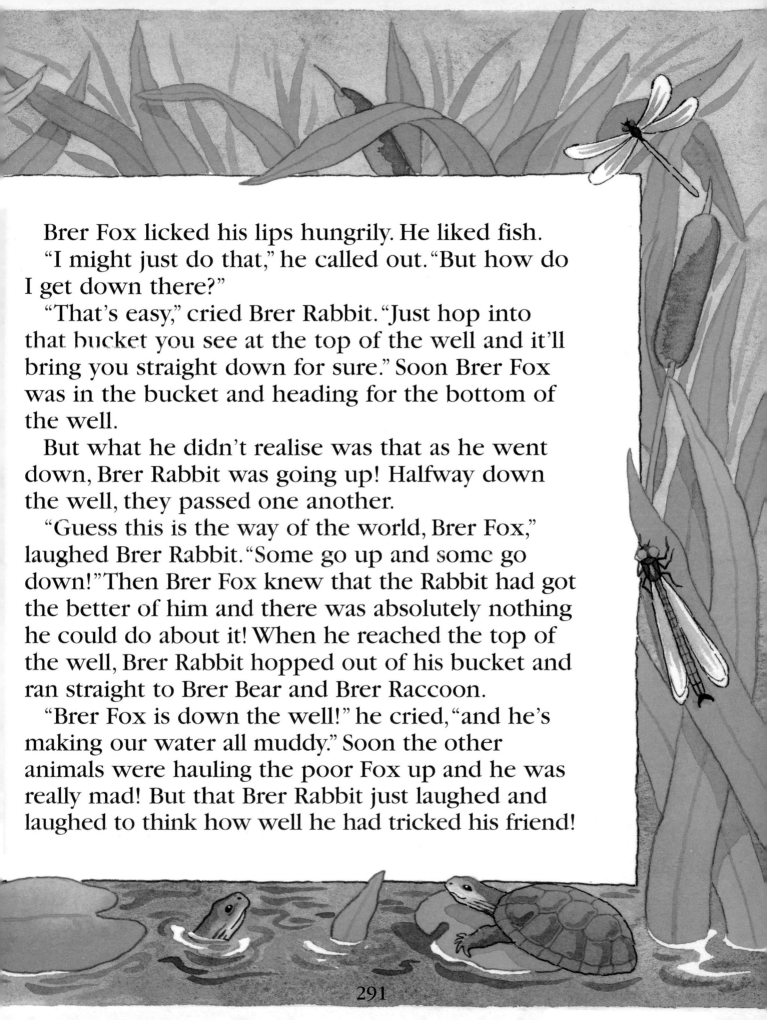

Brer Fox licked his lips hungrily. He liked fish.

"I might just do that," he called out. "But how do I get down there?"

"That's easy," cried Brer Rabbit. "Just hop into that bucket you see at the top of the well and it'll bring you straight down for sure." Soon Brer Fox was in the bucket and heading for the bottom of the well.

But what he didn't realise was that as he went down, Brer Rabbit was going up! Halfway down the well, they passed one another.

"Guess this is the way of the world, Brer Fox," laughed Brer Rabbit. "Some go up and some go down!" Then Brer Fox knew that the Rabbit had got the better of him and there was absolutely nothing he could do about it! When he reached the top of the well, Brer Rabbit hopped out of his bucket and ran straight to Brer Bear and Brer Raccoon.

"Brer Fox is down the well!" he cried, "and he's making our water all muddy." Soon the other animals were hauling the poor Fox up and he was really mad! But that Brer Rabbit just laughed and laughed to think how well he had tricked his friend!

How Miss Cow was Milked

Brer Rabbit was thirsty. He watched Miss Cow grazing peacefully in the meadow. He would love a drink of milk, but how was he to get it? "Howdy, Sis Cow," he said after a while.

"Could you do me a little favor, Sis Cow?" Brer Rabbit went on, all big eyes and innocence.

Miss Cow stopped chewing and looked up at him.

"I would dearly love to eat some of those persimmons," explained Brer Rabbit, pointing to a large tree growing in the meadow. "If you shake the trunk, then they will fall down off the branches and we can share them."

Now Miss Cow was a friendly creature and all too happy to oblige. She ran at that tree full tilt, but what a shock she had when her horn got stuck in the trunk!

Off ran that wily Brer Rabbit and pretty soon he was back with all his little children and each one carried a clanking milk pail! The children clustered so tight around Miss Cow that you could hardly see her and right in the very centre of them sat Brer Rabbit on a three legged stool, milking away for all he was worth.

He filled pail after pail with the sweet warm milk and when he was done he tipped his hat politely.

"I realised you might be stuck there all night and figured that you'd be pretty sore carrying all that milk, so I thought I'd help you out. Kind of a good deed, you might say," and with that he set off for home.

Miss Cow was furious! With one mighty moo, she pawed at the ground and pulled her horn free. Why, she was so mad that Brer Rabbit could have sworn he saw real steam coming from her nostrils!

She raced down the meadow after him and the earth trembled under her hooves. But at the bottom of the field was a large bramble patch and that lucky Rabbit was soon safe inside the bushes. How he laughed.

"There isn't one animal I know who can get the better of ole Brer Rabbit!" he boasted happily.

BRER RABBIT'S GOOD CHILDREN

Brer Fox was hungry. His tummy was a-rumbling and a-grumbling and he knew the only way to quieten it was to find some food. "I wonder if Brer Rabbit has any tasty titbits hidden away inside his house?" Brer Fox wondered and he peeked inside the window. There he saw Brer Rabbit's children frisking about their hole without a care in the world. The hungry Fox licked his lips.

He knew that the little rabbits were all alone because he had just seen Brer Rabbit and Mrs Rabbit inspecting Brer Turtle's cabbage patch. He tapped on the glass with his paw.

"Let me in," called Brer Fox in a wheedling voice, "and I'll just sit and wait for your ole daddy to come home." Now these little rabbits knew Brer Fox and they were polite little rabbits, so they opened the door and pretty soon Brer Fox was sitting comfortably and watching them with a strange look in his eye.

Presently he pointed at a large piece of sugar cane leaning up against the wall.

"I sure am hungry," he said. "Break me off a piece of that cane, will you?" Now Brer Fox knew there isn't anything much tougher in the world than sugar cane and he hoped the rabbits would fail, for then he would have an excuse to eat them. The little bunnies pushed and pulled at the cane but it wouldn't even bend. Just then they heard a bird on the roof singing to them.

"Use your toofies and gnaw it and then it will break."

So the rabbits set to with their sharp teeth and soon they laid a sweet, juicy piece of cane at Brer Fox's feet.

Brer Fox thought again. He would have to find them something harder to do. Then he saw a sieve on the wall.

"I'm mighty thirsty, rabbits!" said he. "Take that sieve and fetch me some water from the spring." The rabbits ran down and dipped the sieve in the water, but to their dismay the water just trickled straight out again. Then they heard the little bird singing once again.

"Line it with clay, then the water will stay."
The rabbits did as they were told and soon they had carried a sieve full of water back to Brer Fox. He was furious to see that this plan had also failed.

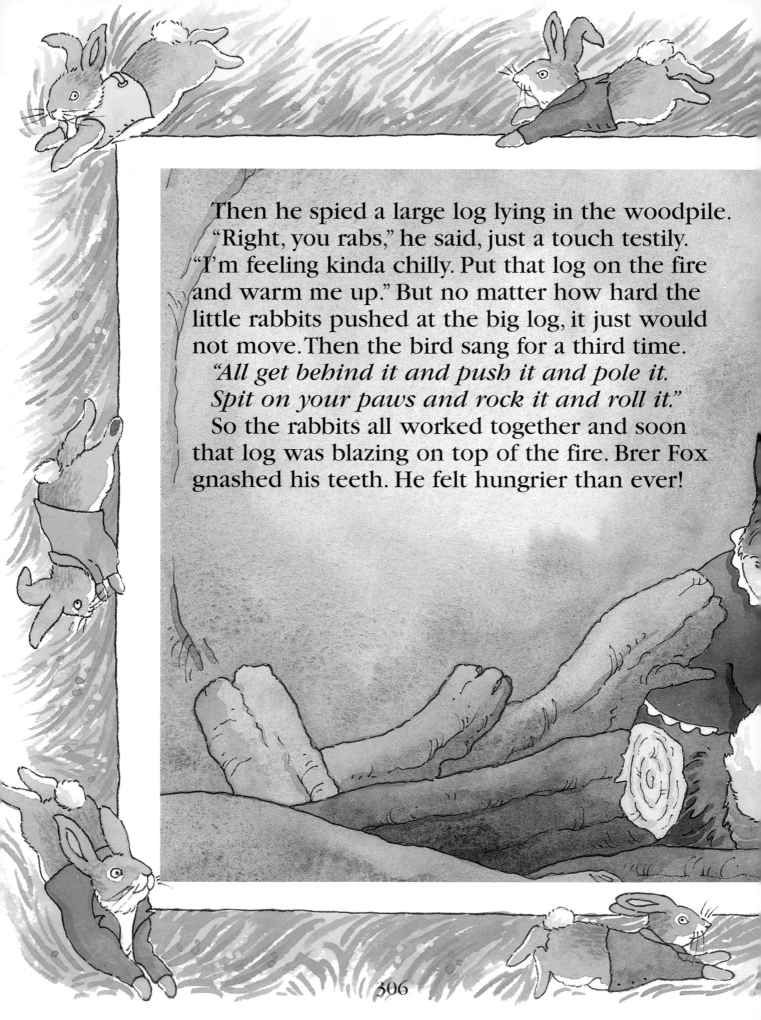

Then he spied a large log lying in the woodpile. "Right, you rabs," he said, just a touch testily. "I'm feeling kinda chilly. Put that log on the fire and warm me up." But no matter how hard the little rabbits pushed at the big log, it just would not move. Then the bird sang for a third time.

"All get behind it and push it and pole it.
Spit on your paws and rock it and roll it."

So the rabbits all worked together and soon that log was blazing on top of the fire. Brer Fox gnashed his teeth. He felt hungrier than ever!

Just then who should walk in but Brer Rabbit himself and my, how his little children were pleased to see him. He took just one look at Brer Fox and knew straightaway what he was up to.

"Do stay and have tea with us, Brer Fox," offered Brer Rabbit. "You look mighty peckish." But something in Brer Rabbit's voice made Brer Fox want to get out of the house as quickly as possible and with a sheepish grin he made his excuses and left.

FISHING FOR THE MOON

One day Brer Rabbit decided to play a trick on his friends, Brer Fox, Brer Wolf and Brer Bear. "I'll invite them to meet us down at the millpond tomorrow evening and we'll go fishing," he told Brer Turtle. The next night the animals set off with their nets and rods and maggots.

But when they got to the pond Brer Rabbit gasped in amazement, then shook his head.

"I reckon they'll be no fishing for us tonight," he said, "for the moon has fallen in the water."

Sure enough, there she lay quivering in the pond and the animals all tut-tutted and scratched their heads.

"Only way we'll get some fishing done tonight is if we drag her out," said Brer Rabbit at last.

"Good idea!" agreed Brer Turtle and soon Brer Fox, Brer Bear and Brer Wolf were in the pond with a net.

"You've nearly got her!" cried Brer Rabbit as he tried hard not to laugh.

"We just can't seem to catch her!" wailed Brer Fox. Deeper and deeper they went until suddenly they were out of their depth and thrashing the water so much it was a wonder they didn't empty the pond! At last they scrambled onto the bank, quite miserable.

"Better luck next time!" said Brer Rabbit grinning broadly and he winked at Brer Turtle. Why, it was almost *too* easy to trick those silly animals!

BRER RABBIT AND THE PEANUT PATCH

Brer Fox was mighty proud of his peanut patch. He weeded it and watered it and looked forward very much to the day when he could eat a fine crop of nuts. But Brer Rabbit had his eye on that self same peanut patch and one morning, when the peanuts had grown big and ripe, he crept through the fence and helped himself just as sassy as you please.

When Brer Fox saw that somebody had been scrabbling in and out of his plants he grew mighty mad.

316

"I'm going to make a trap and catch that no-good varmint who's stealing my peanuts if it's the last thing I do," he said to himself. Soon he had made a fine trap with some rope and a slim hickory sapling and he positioned it right next to the hole in the fence.

The very next day Brer Rabbit came sashaying down the road towards the peanut patch. He wriggled all unsuspecting through the hole in the fence and what a fright he got when he suddenly found himself whisked up in the air and dangling by his back paws on the end of a rope! There he swung, to and fro, while he tried his best to think of a way to free himself.

Just then Brer Bear came ambling down the road. "Howdy, Brer Bear!" called Brer Rabbit.

"What in tarnation are you doin' up there?" asked the astonished Bear as he spotted Brer Rabbit above him.

"Why, I'm earning a dollar a minute guarding the peanut patch for Brer Fox," replied the wily Rabbit. "But I reckon I've earned enough money now," he added. "Do you want to take over from me?"

Brer Bear looked at him doubtfully. "Do you reckon I could do it?" he said. Brer Rabbit nodded encouragingly.

"Why, it's easy as pie," he said. "I'll show you what to do!"

Soon Brer Rabbit was standing on the ground and Brer Bear was swinging in the air.

"Brer Fox, come out!" shouted the naughty Rabbit. "Here's the rascal who's been stealing your peanuts!" Out shot Brer Fox with a stout stick in his hand.

"So that's your game, is it?" he cried, and he set about poor Brer Bear with his stick. The Bear tried in vain to explain that he was guarding his peanut patch for him but the furious Brer Fox did not believe a single word of it.

And where was Brer Rabbit? Why, he was long gone. Long gone!

Tales of the Arabian Nights

These tales were first heard many hundreds of years ago and are part of one of the greatest story collections of all time: *The Tales of the Arabian Nights*. The story goes that they were originally told by the beautiful Princess Scheherezade to the suspicious Prince of Tartary, who had threatened to behead her at daybreak. But her tales were so exciting that, as the sun rose, he longed to hear how they ended and so pardoned her life for one more day, until after one thousand and one nights Scheherezade had won his trust and his heart.

Illustrated by Helen Cockburn

Aladdin and the Magic Lamp

O nce upon a time there lived a lazy boy called Aladdin. His father was dead and his poor mother despaired of her good-for-nothing son ever finding himself a job for he spent all his time running around the street markets and teasing the stallholders. One day a stranger approached him.

"Are you Aladdin?" he asked, and the boy nodded.

"I am your father's brother and have been away for a long time," explained the man. "Now I am back and would like to give you work." When Aladdin's mother heard this news she was overjoyed and welcomed the stranger to their home. But what the trusting woman did not know was that this was no uncle but a scheming magician who was looking for a boy to help him.

"I will buy you some new clothes," said the pretend uncle to Aladdin, "and then you must come with me on a short journey." The next day they walked for many miles into the country and soon the town was left far behind. The boy's feet ached and he longed to go back.

"We are here," said the magician at last and he made a small fire. Throwing on some strange powders, he chanted a magic spell and the earth trembled under their feet. To Aladdin's astonishment a stone slab appeared in the ground. The magician pulled it back to reveal a flight of steps leading down and out of sight.

"You are to follow the steps into a secret garden and there you will find a lamp," said the magician. "Bring it to me and I will reward you well." Then he gave the boy a ring. "Wear this for protection," he said.

The Garden was full of beautiful trees sparkling with the strangest fruit Aladdin had ever seen.

"I will take some home with me," he said, then he found the lamp and returned to the top of the steps.

"Hand me the lamp and you can come out," ordered the magician and his eyes glittered cruelly. Aladdin shivered. He did not trust this man.

"First give me my reward," he insisted. The magician had not expected this and he flew into a rage.

"Do you not know who I am, you foolish boy?" he cried and he slammed the stone slab shut. Then the angry magician fled far away to Africa, leaving poor Aladdin trapped in the dark cave. For two whole days the boy wept bitterly then at last he fell to his knees and prayed for help. His fingers rubbed the ring and suddenly a huge genie appeared in front of him.

"What is your wish?" thundered the genie. "I am the Slave of the Ring and will obey you in all things."

Aladdin lost no time in wishing to be taken home and soon found himself back with his mother.

"Why would the wicked man want this dirty old lamp?" she wondered and she gave it a rub.

With a huge flash, another enormous genie appeared and bowed low before them.

"I am the Genie of the Lamp!" he cried. "Your wish is my command!" Quickly Aladdin ordered food and drink and soon he and his mother were eating off silver dishes. Then Aladdin showed his mother the strange fruit that he had picked.

"This is no fruit, my son," she gasped. "These are the biggest jewels I have ever seen. We are rich, rich!"

"And look at these fine silver plates, mother," said Aladdin. "We can sell these and need never worry about money again." So they hid the jewels and sold the plates and lived happily for many months.

Now the ruler of this country was a mighty Sultan and he had a lovely daughter. On certain days she would go to bathe in the springs of a lovely garden close by Aladdin's home. It was forbidden to look at the Princess as she passed by but Aladdin was filled with a desire to see her face. One day he hid behind the gate and caught a glimpse of her as she passed by.

The Princess was so beautiful that Aladdin fell in love with her there and then. He had to win her heart!

"The Princess would never marry you!" laughed his mother. "She will want to marry a rich Prince." But Aladdin begged her to visit the palace and ask the Sultan's permission.

"You can give him our jewels as a gift," he added.

When the Sultan saw the jewels his eyes lit up.

"Any man who owns such riches as these must be deserving of my daughter's hand," he said. But his chief minister, the Grand Vizier, was most displeased for he wanted the Princess to marry his own son.

"You must set the young man a difficult task to fulfil," he advised. "He must prove that he is worthy of the Princess." Then the Sultan rubbed his chin thoughtfully.

"Tell your son he must bring me forty basins of gold, overflowing with jewels, and they must be carried by forty strong slaves," he said at last. When Aladdin heard this he rubbed the magic lamp and the genie burst forth from the spout and bowed low. The very instant that Aladdin made his request, his house became full of jostling slaves, each carrying a bowl of fine jewels.

Aladdin's mother led the way to the palace and when the Sultan saw the procession he was lost for words.

"This must be a very wealthy man indeed," he thought to himself and he happily gave permission for Aladdin to marry his daughter. At once the happy boy began his preparations. With another quick polish of the lamp he summoned the genie.

"I need a set of clothes fit for a Prince," he said, "and then you can build me a palace for us to live in." The new palace was magnificent. The walls were gold and silver and the windows were surrounded by diamonds.

Soon Aladdin and the Princess were man and wife.

But far away in Africa the magician had not forgotten the magic lamp and after several years had passed he returned to the city to seek it out. The first thing he saw was the grand new palace twinkling in the sun.

"That is where Prince Aladdin and his bride live," an old man told him. "The Prince is the richest man for miles around." The magician ground his teeth in rage for he knew that the lamp had won him this wealth.

One day Aladdin left on a hunting trip and while he was away the magician thought of a plan. He disguised himself as a peddler and arrived at the palace gate with a basket full of shiny new copper lamps.

"I will swap my new lamps for your old lamps!" he cried, and the Princess heard him from her window.

"What a strange idea!" she laughed. "Take him this dirty old lamp if he wants it," and, not knowing its value, she handed her maid the magic lamp.

"Would you take this old lamp?" the maid asked the magician and the wicked man nearly shouted for joy. Quickly he grabbed the lamp and sped from the city. As night fell he rubbed the spout and roused the genie.

"Take the Princess and her palace back to Africa with me," he ordered, and in a flash it was done. The next day the Sultan was horrified to find that the palace and his beloved daughter had disappeared.

"Aladdin has tricked you!" cried the Grand Vizier. Then the enraged Sultan ordered that Aladdin be captured and put to death. When the townspeople heard the news they were angry and shouted out for Aladdin's release. The Sultan hesitated for the Prince was very popular. At last he decided to show mercy.

"I swear to you that I will find the Princess," the boy promised when he was found. "If I should fail then you can punish me however you like."

So Aladdin's life was spared and he left the city to seek his wife. But it was as if she had disappeared into thin air. No-one knew where she was and no-one could help him. Many days passed by and at last he threw himself on his knees and prayed. As he did so, he rubbed the magic ring he still wore on his finger. With a flash of light the genie appeared before him.

"Take me to the Princess," begged the delighted Aladdin and in a trice he found himself outside her window. Soon she was in his arms and telling him all that had happened. Then Aladdin understood. The Genie of the Lamp had a new master. Carefully he handed the Princess a small packet of powder.

"Pour this poison into the magician's wine," he said, "and all our troubles will be over." They could hear the wicked man approaching so Aladdin quickly hid.

"Do have a glass of wine," urged the Princess to the magician, then she waited until his back was turned and tipped the powder into his glass. Sure enough, with the very next sip of his wine, the magician fell lifeless to the floor. Then Aladdin burst from his hiding place and found the lamp inside the magician's coat.

"Your true master has returned," he told the Genie. "Now take us back home!" And so Aladdin lived happily ever after and wherever he went he always took great care to keep his magic lamp well hidden!

Ali Baba and the Forty Thieves

Far away in the land of Persia there lived two brothers, Ali Baba and Cassim. Ali Baba was a poor man but Cassim was wealthy and lived in a fine house with plenty to eat and drink. Sadly, his wife was a greedy woman and always wanted more.

Ali Baba was chopping firewood in the forest one day when he heard the sound of horse's hooves. He feared that robbers might be coming so scrambled up a tree to safety. Silently he watched as a large body of men rode past and pulled up by a sheer rock face. The leader of the men dismounted and strode up to the rock.

"Open, Sesame!" he cried, and to Ali Baba's great amazement a secret door swung open. Ali Baba counted as the men slipped inside the opening and disappeared from view.

"Forty robbers!" he said to himself. "I wonder what they have hidden inside that cave." Some time later the robbers emerged and galloped away. Then Ali Baba slid down from the tree and stood by the rock face.

"Open, Sesame!" he cried, and lo and behold, the rock door slid open and he quickly ran inside.

Ali Baba expected to find a dark and dismal hole but to his great astonishment the cave was full of the most magnificent treasures. Fine silks lay in bundles upon the floor and exquisite jewels were scattered round about. Great coffers and chests overflowed with gold coins and yet more gold was heaped up in piles around the walls. Ali Baba rubbed his hands with glee! Now he need never go hungry again. Quickly he gathered up as much gold as he could carry and hurried home.

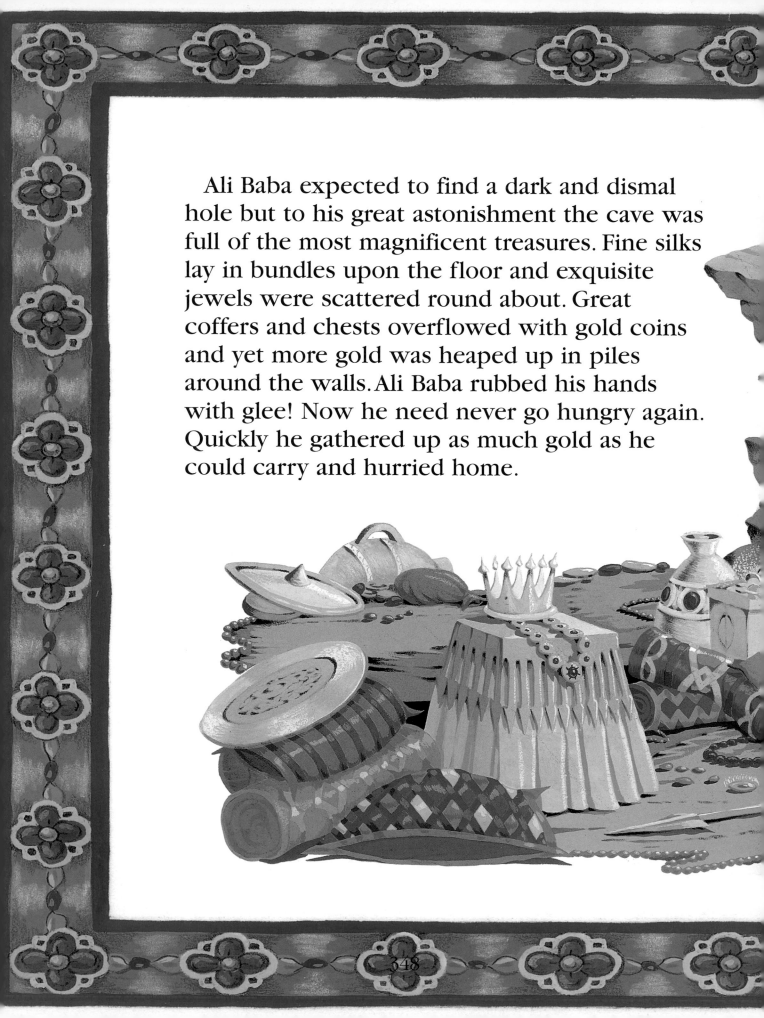

Ali Baba's wife was overjoyed to see the money.

"Please let me weigh it before you hide it away," she begged her husband and she borrowed a set of scales from Cassim and his wife, her nearest neighbours.

"I wonder what she wants them for?" puzzled Cassim's wife. But when the scales were returned to her later she discovered the truth because in her haste, Ali Baba's wife had left one gold piece in the bottom of the pan. Cassim's wife was jealous.

"Ali Baba has so much money he does not bother to *count* it," she told her husband. "He simply *weighs* it!" Then Cassim lost no time in asking Ali Baba where he had found so much gold. Honest Ali Baba explained what he had seen and offered to share the treasure with his brother. But the wily Cassim decided he would go to the cave alone and take all the treasure for himself. Early the next day he set off with his donkeys.

"Open, Sesame!" he cried and, sure enough, the cave door swung open. Hurriedly he filled sack after sack with jewels and gold coins but when he wished to leave he could not remember the magic word to open the door and let him out again

Cassim tried name after name but the door stayed firmly shut. After a while, to his great horror, he heard the trampling of horse's hooves outside the cave.

In rushed the robbers and they fell upon him with their long sabres and cut him into four quarters. Then they left him there as a lesson to any other intruder.

That night Ali Baba went in search of Cassim and what a dreadful sight awaited him when he entered the cave. Sadly, he carried home the four quarters of his body and laid them on the table. Cassim's wife wailed and sobbed but Ali Baba's servant, a clever woman called Morgiana, remained calm.

"I will find a cobbler to stitch the four quarters together," she decided, "and then the body can be buried peacefully." So saying, she set off for the market and there she found an old cobbler hard at work.

"I have a job for you, old man," she whispered, "but you must not breathe a word of it to anyone." Then she tied a blindfold around his head and led him to the house of Ali Baba. The cobbler stitched away at the four quarters and late that night Morgiana blindfolded him once more and led him back to his stall.

When the Forty Thieves returned to their cave they were astonished to find that the body was missing.

"Someone else knows our secret password!" cried the Captain. "He must be found!" One of the robbers was sent to the city to discover all he could and as he entered the city gate the first person he saw was the old cobbler. When the robber offered him a gold coin, the cobbler told him all that had happened.

"I am sure I could find the house again," he said and soon he had led the robber to the very door.

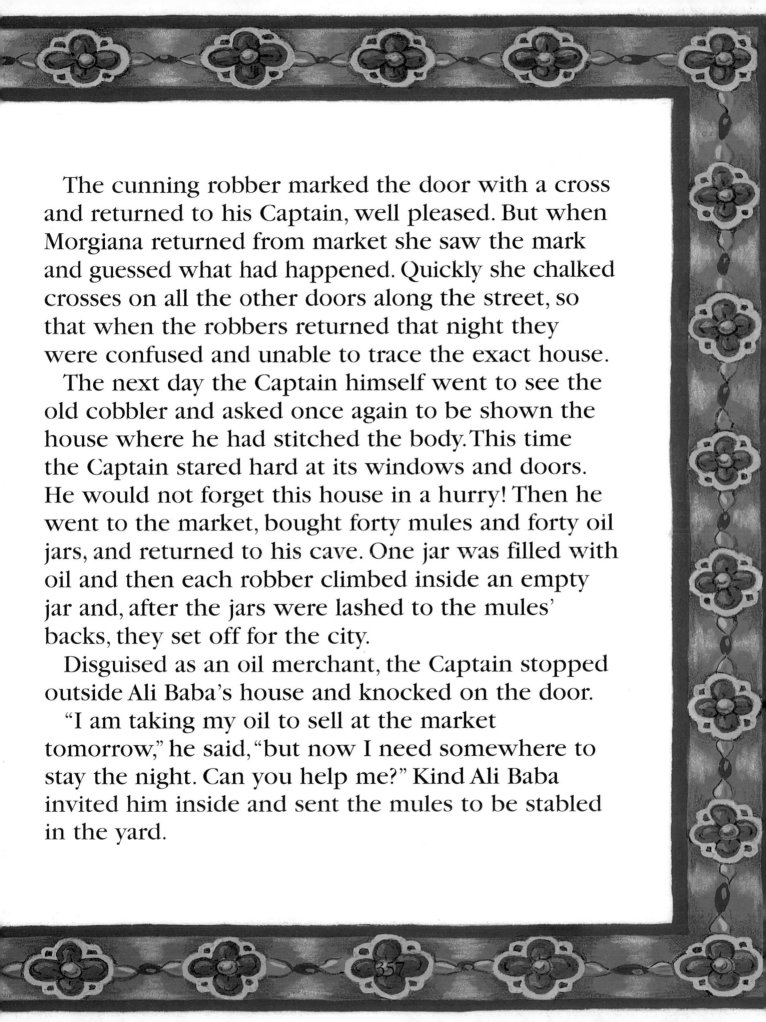

The cunning robber marked the door with a cross and returned to his Captain, well pleased. But when Morgiana returned from market she saw the mark and guessed what had happened. Quickly she chalked crosses on all the other doors along the street, so that when the robbers returned that night they were confused and unable to trace the exact house.

The next day the Captain himself went to see the old cobbler and asked once again to be shown the house where he had stitched the body. This time the Captain stared hard at its windows and doors. He would not forget this house in a hurry! Then he went to the market, bought forty mules and forty oil jars, and returned to his cave. One jar was filled with oil and then each robber climbed inside an empty jar and, after the jars were lashed to the mules' backs, they set off for the city.

Disguised as an oil merchant, the Captain stopped outside Ali Baba's house and knocked on the door.

"I am taking my oil to sell at the market tomorrow," he said, "but now I need somewhere to stay the night. Can you help me?" Kind Ali Baba invited him inside and sent the mules to be stabled in the yard.

Later that night the Captain crept into the yard and whispered his orders to his men, still hiding in the jars.

"Be ready to fight when I give you the word!" he hissed, then tiptoed back inside to join his host. Ali Baba had invited him to join them for a meal and Morgiana was busy cooking in the kitchen.

"I was not expecting visitors," she fussed to herself, "and now I have run out of oil!" Then she remembered the oil jars in the yard. "I am sure the merchant will not mind if a take a little for my cooking," she said to herself as she hurried outside with her jar and lamp. Suddenly she heard a voice — and she was sure it came from inside one of the oil jars!

"Is it time to fight yet, master?" it said. Then Morgiana knew that these were the robbers come to attack her master and, filling her lamp with oil, she quickly ran back inside the house. She boiled a large pan of oil and when it was scalding hot she tipped it over each of the robbers until they were all dead.

At midnight the Captain tried to rouse his robbers but without success. When he discovered each one had been killed he fled over the wall and was gone.

The next morning Morgiana told Ali Baba of all that had happened and he thanked the clever girl for saving his life. But back in the lonely cave, the Robber Captain sat hatching a different plot to kill him.

This time he disguised himself as a rich cloth merchant and set up a stall opposite Ali Baba's house. As the days passed the unsuspecting Ali Baba grew quite friendly with the merchant and invited him to dine at his house.

But as soon as the merchant arrived at the door clever Morgiana knew who it was straight away.

"Fetch your drum!" she told Abdallah, the kitchen servant. "I will dance for my master and his honoured guest." Ali Baba, his son and the pretend merchant lay upon silk cushions on the floor. As the drum beat grew louder, Morgiana whirled around the room, each time coming ever closer to the wicked Robber Captain.

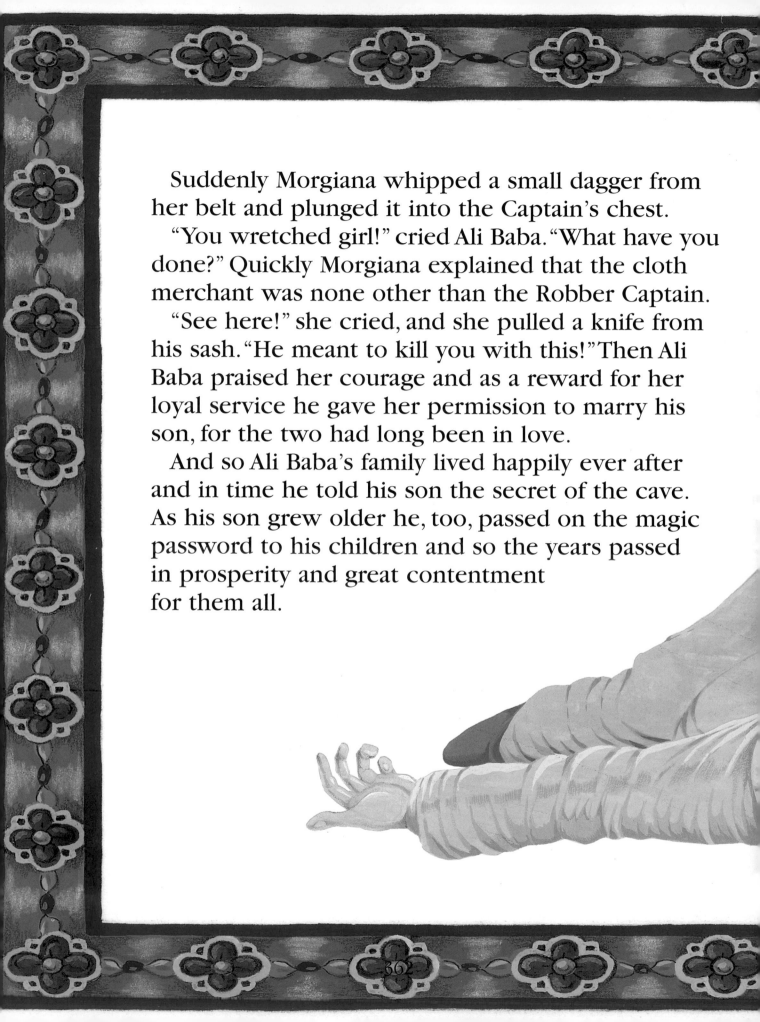

Suddenly Morgiana whipped a small dagger from her belt and plunged it into the Captain's chest.

"You wretched girl!" cried Ali Baba. "What have you done?" Quickly Morgiana explained that the cloth merchant was none other than the Robber Captain.

"See here!" she cried, and she pulled a knife from his sash. "He meant to kill you with this!" Then Ali Baba praised her courage and as a reward for her loyal service he gave her permission to marry his son, for the two had long been in love.

And so Ali Baba's family lived happily ever after and in time he told his son the secret of the cave. As his son grew older he, too, passed on the magic password to his children and so the years passed in prosperity and great contentment for them all.

Sinbad the Sailor

This is the story of Sinbad the Sailor and his many strange adventures across the far seas. His first voyage was on a merchant ship bound for the East Indies and one day it passed a peculiar little island. It was smooth and green and the Captain decided his sailors could go ashore and stretch their legs. But when the cook lit a fire the earth began to tremble beneath their feet and to their horror, the whole island rose up out of the water and everyone was thrown into the sea.

"It is a whale!" shouted the Captain. "Swim for the ship!" He quickly weighed anchor and set sail, but one sailor was left behind and that was Sinbad! He clung to a piece of driftwood and watched as the ship slowly disappeared from sight. Two days passed before the waves pushed him close to the shores of an island.

Soon he was lying upon dry land.

"I must find water and food," he gasped and set off into the forest that bordered the beach. He had not gone far when he found an extraordinary white dome lying upon the ground. What could it be?

Just then Sinbad heard the flapping of wings high above him and glancing up he saw the most enormous bird. It was a Roc and the strange dome must surely be the Roc's egg! Sure enough she landed close by and sat down upon her nest. Then Sinbad had an idea.

"If I tie myself to her foot I may be able to escape from this island," he thought and he quickly wrapped his turban around one huge claw. At daybreak the Roc stood up and with a mighty cry took off into the sky. She flew over sea, then over land and at last swooped down and came to rest in a deep valley. Sinbad hastily untied himself and looked around.

To his amazement he found the ground was covered with glittering diamonds. Just then Sinbad heard a hiss and spinning around he saw six large serpents slithering across the rocks towards him. He turned and ran and at last found a hiding place in a hole in the ground. There he hid all that day and all through the night and at last the serpents gave up and crawled away.

Suddenly a a huge lump of meat fell on the ground in front of him. Then another, and another. With a loud flapping of wings a great eagle landed on one large piece of meat and took off into the air again. Sinbad remembered a story he had heard about the men who lived in these parts. They had devised a special way of gathering diamonds. They threw meat down into the valley and the jewels would stick to the soft flesh. Then the eagles would grab the meat and fly with it to their nests. There the hunters picked the diamonds from the meat and so both eagles and men were happy! Quickly Sinbad tied himself to a piece of meat. This could be his way out of the valley! Sure enough, an eagle took the meat and flew off to his nest. What a shock the hunter got to see a man landing there!

From the mountain top Sinbad found his way to
the coast and set sail once again but this time his
ship was blown off course by a violent wind.
They came close to an island and saw to their
horror that the sea was full of strange monkey-
like creatures swimming towards them. Soon they
were crawling on the decks and swarming up
the rigging.

The Ape Men took over the ship and forced Sinbad and his shipmates to jump overboard and swim for land. They set off to explore the island and soon found a deserted palace. In the courtyard was a huge mound of what looked suspiciously like human bones but the men were so tired that they decided to rest there for the night. Suddenly a loud roar filled the air and in through the gate strode the most horrible one-eyed ogre. The sailors sat rooted to the spot.

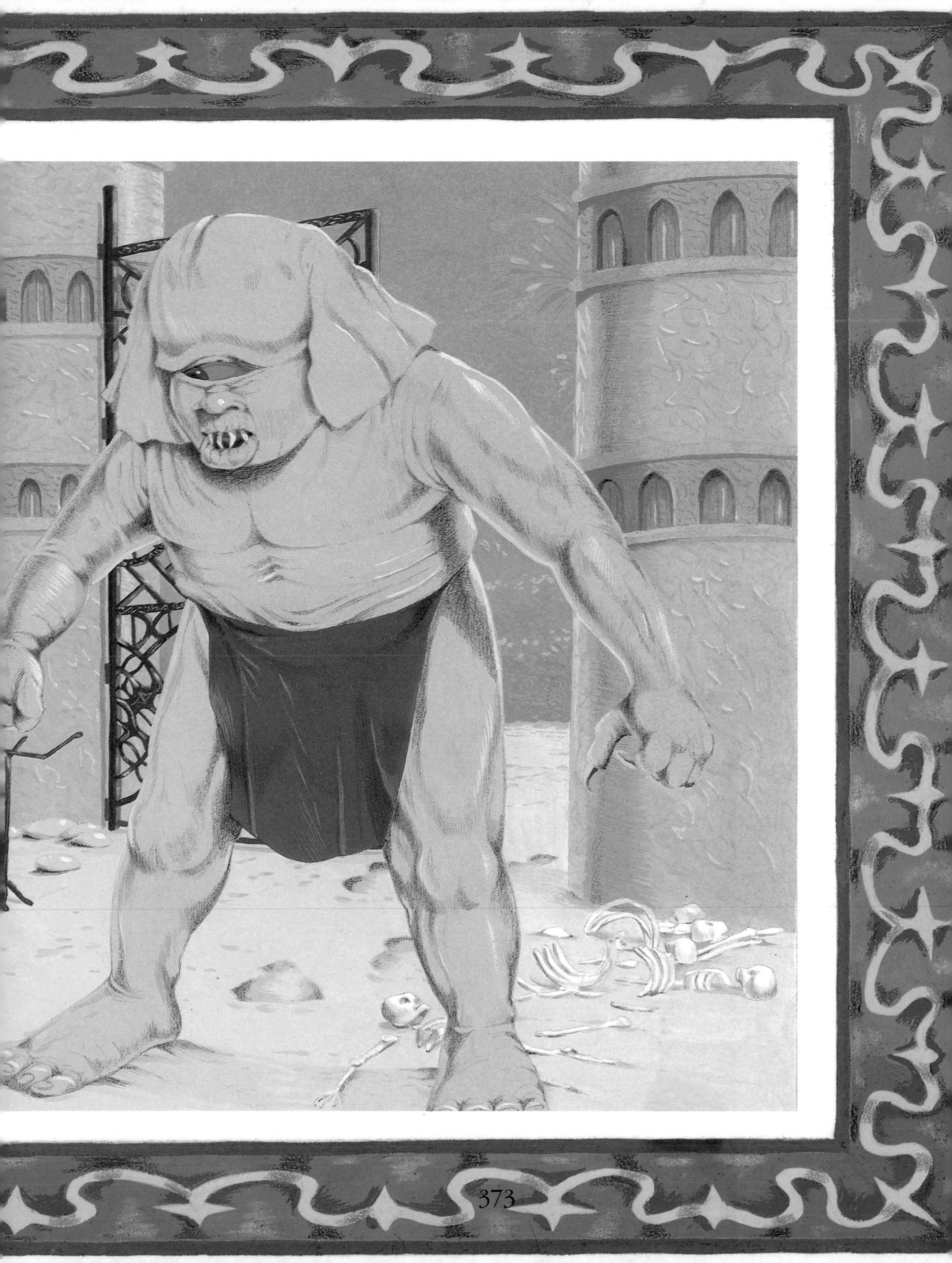

The beast plucked up one sailor and while the others watched in horror, roasted him on a spit and with much smacking of lips, ate him! Then the ogre fell asleep and his huge body blocked the gateway.

"We must try and kill him," whispered Sinbad. "If we take the red hot spits from the fire and push them in his eye he will surely die." So they crept up on the giant as he lay on his back and thrust the iron poles into his eye. The giant howled with pain and the sailors quickly made their escape. But the ogre was not dead and he chased them through the jungle and down to the beach. The terrified men leapt into the sea and swam for their lives while the ogre threw huge boulders after them. Many perished but lucky Sinbad survived with two other sailors.

At last the waves threw them upon another island and there another danger awaited them. A giant green lizard crept from the bushes and before they knew what was upon them, had gobbled down Sinbad's companions. Clever Sinbad lit a circle of fire around a tall tree then climbed into its branches. That night he was safe from the fearsome beast.

The next morning he saw a ship sail close by and, jumping from the tree he ran into the sea, shouting at the top of his voice. To his great relief, the Captain heard him and had soon pulled him on board.

After this Sinbad spent some time at home but after many months had passed he set sail once again. This time the ship ran out of food and the hungry sailors landed upon an unknown shore and set off in search of something to eat. To their delight they found a baby Roc hatching from its huge shell.

"Do not touch it!" cried Sinbad. "The mother Roc is a huge bird and will surely kill you," but the sailors paid him no heed and soon the infant Roc was roasting over a fire. Then the sky above them went dark and looking up, the sailors were horrified to see both mother and father Roc returning to their egg.

"To the ship! To the ship!" they cried as they ran pell mell down the beach. Soon the ship was fleeing the island, but the Rocs were in full pursuit. They bore huge rocks which they dropped upon the hapless sailors and soon the sea was full of drowning men. Good fortune was smiling again on Sinbad, for he was the only survivor.

At last the sea cast him upon an island and Sinbad set off to explore inland. He had not gone far when he came upon an old man sitting beside a brook.

"Please carry me across to the fruit trees on the other side," asked the old man pitifully. Sinbad gladly obliged but was shocked to find that the old man wrapped his legs around Sinbad's neck so strongly that he nearly passed out and at last fell down upon the ground. Then the old man gave him a mighty kick in the ribs and forced him up and onwards. All that day the old man ate fruit after fruit and at night he slept with his legs still locked tightly around Sinbad's head.

So it went on, day after day, and at last Sinbad thought of a plan. He squeezed a good amount of grape juice into an empty gourd and left it in the sun. After a while the juice turned into wine and Sinbad offered it to the old man.

"This is good," said the old man, swallowing it eagerly, and soon the gourd was empty. But the old man was drunk and danced so happily upon Sinbad's shoulders that he soon fell off! So at last Sinbad was free. Once again he hailed a passing ship and scrambled aboard.

After a time the ship landed at an island well known for its wonderful coconuts.

"This is how you gather them," a rich merchant told Sinbad. "Just copy me." Then he began throwing stones at the monkeys who clustered around the nuts at the top of the palm trees. The angry monkeys grabbed the nearest missiles to hand and soon coconuts were raining down upon the ground!

Sinbad traded his coconuts for spices and silks on his voyage around the islands but his next journey was to end once again in calamity. His ship was caught in a strong current which dragged it upon sharp rocks and the sailors were cast screaming overboard.

Sinbad found himself the sole survivor upon that rocky coast but there seemed to be no escape.

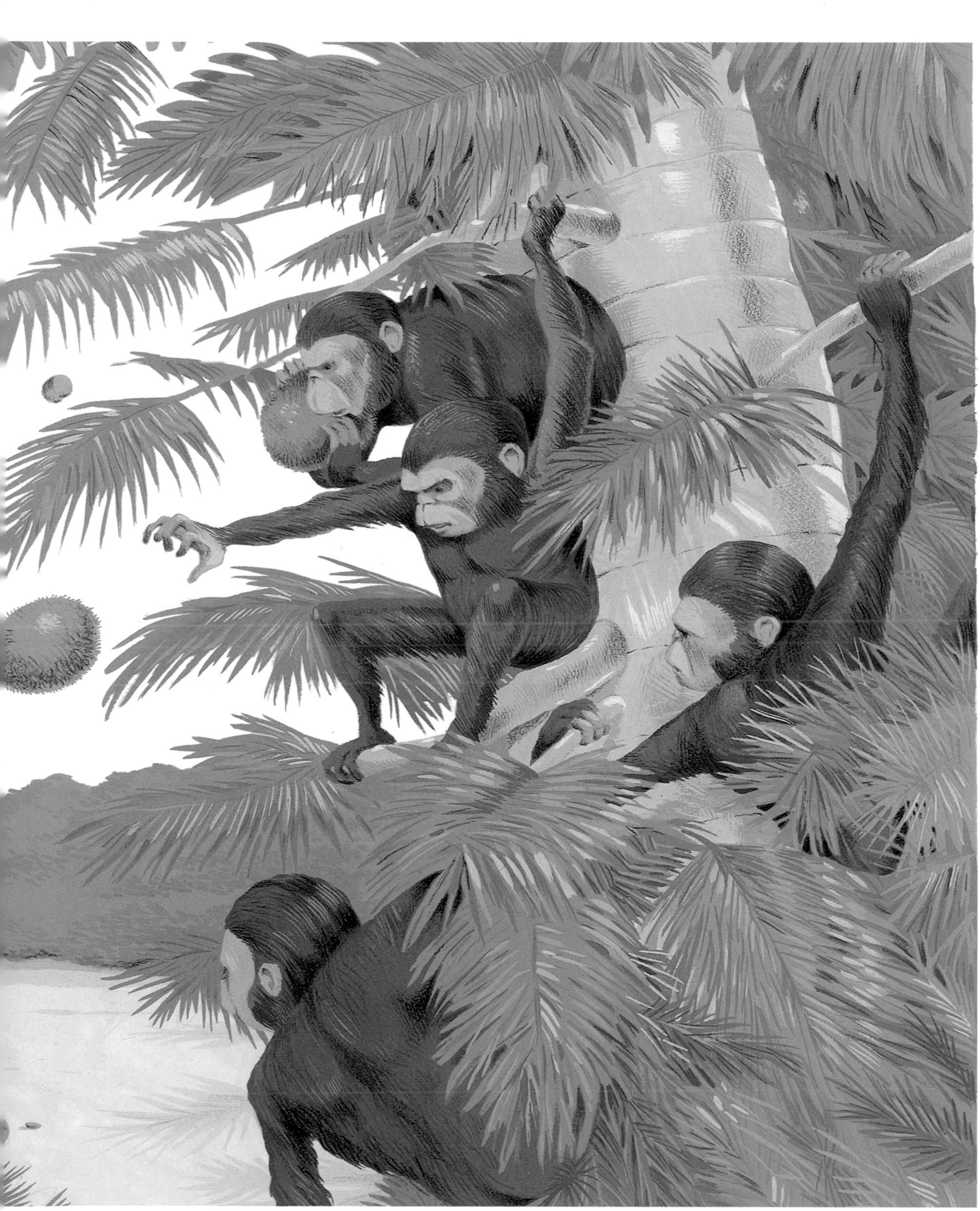

At last he found a small channel cut through the sheer rock face where the sea had forced a passage inland. He made himself a raft and, lashing himself to the timbers, set sail under the mountain. The current carried him through the dark for many hours but at last he emerged into bright sunshine and was found by a group of natives. They led him before their King and soon Sinbad was recounting his many exciting voyages to far off lands. The King was fascinated.

"Please return to your Sultan with gifts from the island of Serendib," he said, "but be sure to return soon for I would dearly love to hear more of your adventures."

So Sinbad arrived home with many costly presents which the Sultan was well pleased to receive.

"Now you must visit the King again," the Sultan told Sinbad. "We must repay his generosity with gifts of our own." So it was that Sinbad returned to the island of Serendib and was treated like a royal visitor.

At last he made his final farewells and set sail for home. He was getting old and wished to spend the rest of his days in the safe harbour of his house, surrounded by loving family and friends. The voyages of Sinbad the Sailor were over!

Goodnight!